Guardians at the Gate

RAY DACOLIAS

Guardians at the Gate

ISBN 978-0-9888177-6-0

Contents

Margaret

She had been raised on the singular notion that men were the tangled root of all evil for women, and she was nourished on a strict diet of fresh carcasses of those men around her who seemed to fail her mother, her grandmother, her sister and herself. This, however, did not impede her trespass into matrimony with a man, a deed done if only to verify for herself that men were, as a race, a savage crop of unrepentant, stinking brutes who had victimized and tortured women from time immemorial.

She married three times to continuously test her hypothesis that men were indeed scoundrels, and each time she decided she was correct. "Margaret," her mother once said to her, after observing her own husband's drunken and sprawled form on the wooden floor, "a man's ability to show love is like a dog walking on its hind legs; baby, it is not done well, but you are surprised to find it done at all." Her female mistresses were sure to accentuate numerous instances where the worst of Man was magnified and then scrutinized and ingested by her; and so, just as a mother bird feeds worms to her starving chicks, the final distillation of Man's failures was daily thrown down Margaret's eager throat. Thus, she, at a very early age, seemed to have been inoculated against the possibility of a man's love ever entering her delicate heart.

She begrudgingly gave birth to three males, each time evincing a sour expression on her pained countenance as the gender of the baby was announced to her.

By the time her boys had reached manhood, only one of them would survive his relationship with his mother, and that son, the youngest, never strayed far from the taut umbilical cord that seemed to extend from his sinking manhood to his mother's soothing belly.

Target Practice

Words in a bad marriage are like the tiny splinters of a bullet that have slowly accumulated in a person's body over the years; with each carefully aimed verbal missile fired at a spouse, the splinters collect inside the poor recipient until they coagulate into what the body perceives as a real object. Now, this verbal bullet sits, depending on the severity and duration of the splinters that formed it, near this organ or that, moving closer each day down a slippery slope as its antagonist continues to shoot auxiliary shrapnel onto its sinewy tracks.

One black, foggy night, Margaret let loose a gruesome shout against her first husband that sank so fast and deep into his debilitated body that it landed atop a special verbal bullet which she had some years past shot into the fragile cavities of his heart. He was dead the next day, having survived ten years with a woman who had ground his resistance down just as if he were a mountain and she were a steam shovel that had gulped large amounts of soil every day from his teetering foundation.

It was as if it was her instinct to take down any man who was in a traditional position of power over woman. It was her second husband, realizing this about her, who once remarked, "By Jove, she'll be fighting every man alive! Doesn't she know that?" and upon further reflection, he said to himself, rather soberly, "By my own blood and fear, I believe she does."

After the death of her third husband, she said, gravely, sitting down one day with her precious youngest boy, Roger, "No natural woman will ever suffer abuse at the hands of a man as long as I can still breathe."

"Yes, Mama," her dutiful son had replied, holding her strong hand for strength.

When she was first married, she refused to allow her husband to support her financially. "I'm not going to let any man keep me down," she often said to herself. "But I must choose a profession wisely, one in which I can influence our nation's girls to become Independent Women."

As it was, she became an elementary school teacher, and this is really where our story, albeit coyly, begins.

Schools

Public schools are a universe unto themselves, and no foreigner—that is to say, any outsider—may comment on its curious society with any accurate intelligence.

There are a finite number of questions regarding the educational system, such as: have outsiders, for centuries, been drawn to a false conclusion about public schools? Is it possible that our schools are run like private businesses, where school leaders treat their Teachers simply as antagonists who must take orders and where the children are simply units whose success is encouraged so the executives of the schools may prosper economically and socially? Or is it that schools are open communities where children and parents and educators celebrate the joy of learning, and the school officials act as doting parents solicitous of their employees and pupils?

It is through Margaret C. Carbuncle, who would retain the surname of her last husband for the remainder of her life, that we shall examine the intimate inner workings of public schools.

Now, let us commence with our story with a bit more resolve.

Our School

There is a school district in the lower extremities of southern California that sits snugly in the middle of a growing community of cities. Gentle breezes and sunny days and sloping hills are the idyllic environs for the Green Valley Unified School District.

Sapphire Elementary is one such school in this district, a school deriving its name from the street upon which it was built, and the street having derived its name from the precious bright blue mineral, sapphire.

Margaret Carbuncle worked at Sapphire Elementary. She taught sixth grade to children who came from a broad spectrum of lower- and middle-class divisions. Inherent in these socioeconomic classes were further subdivisions involving education of parents, and the mental health and emotional stability and moral value of each family. As it was, the students in her class were like young saplings putting out brightly colored buds that reached toward the yellow, nourishing sun, turning eagerly toward their Teacher for knowledge and guidance.

But Margaret Carbuncle would have none of that.

Black and white are much easier colors to follow in regard to rules and regulations and orders than any color of gray that might weave its nebulous self into unknown and uncomfortable territories. It is sometimes said, by certain Teachers, that they teach only those basic core contents needed by their students to attain the next grade level; yet, implicit in such a statement is that there are special lessons that offer delicious minutes designed to flame the fires of desire for knowledge within each student. But Margaret balked at such nonsense. She needed a strict set of guidelines placed before her so she might follow them—and those with no humor, no augmentation, no magic transposed onto the readily adhered-to plan from her at all, to wit:

Her students stood in one long, straight line, ranked by their intellectual order—a ranking procured by rigorous testing Margaret put them through—outside her classroom, and the order varied day to day according to her rigorous and lengthy testing; the students were not allowed to enter the room until their posture was perfect and their hands held still behind their backs and their faces free of emotional frivolity. And what if it was exceedingly hot or exceedingly cold outside? Then her students were there, boiling in the sun and melting like soft chocolate on the burning concrete or feeling the icy wind cut to their small bones until every one of them was absolutely still and absolutely quiet; when the students did walk into the room, they knew exactly where to go and what to do and how to sit—they put away their personal material and homework and proceeded on the carefully laid-out assignments on their desk and sat fully erect; as the morning progressed, no voice was heard in the room except that of Margaret, and if a student was allowed to speak, it was in a fashion after her; there was no movement in the room, except that of Margaret, and if there was movement in the room by a student, it was in a way that had been carefully defined and laid out by her; there was no free will in the room, except that of Margaret, and if a student happened to utter an extemporaneous comment, it had to reflect her will; if there was a query from a student, the student wrote it down and deposited it in a small straw basket on the top left-hand corner of their desk; if they dropped a pencil, a paper, a book, they did not move toward it, but raised their hand and used special sign language taught to them by their lady and mistress to indicate their desire to retrieve the dropped item; if they wished to go to the bathroom, they wished it away, lest it cost them dire consequences in the form of an after-school detention and a sign with a string that was draped over their chest that declared as they walked around campus, "Baby on board—I am incapable of comprehending the need to visit the bathroom when necessary."

Her students had lunch in her room. "They are here for an education, not for gossip," she often said to her embarrassed colleagues. Her students never engaged in physical education. "Every minute is an instructional minute—let them run around like savages at their homes," she more than once remarked to her incredulous colleagues. Her students stayed after school every day for two hours. "The only way to get ahead is to labor hard when you are young, when your peers are loafers and unaware of the horrors to come," she took great pride in saying to anyone who would listen.

When she taught, she taught only those items that could be measured on a standardized test; thus, her scores were high and her administrators heaped praise upon her just as if she were a hero returning from a long battle. "Receiving high test scores is not difficult—I don't care what the students want, or if they enjoy my class or like me, or even if they are learning what they ought, it is what the state wants them to know for the test," she relished relating to her Principal.

So, there it is—between the covers of a book, she never saw anything but the exact words and their exact meaning: nothing inferred, nothing imagined, nothing colored nor adventures realized; what was there was there to her and was safe and known and easily explained. Such thinking patterns, within any school system, naturally lead one to consider the attainment of an administrative credential, which often recruits such minds that inhabit a dull universe where there is no room nor color nor music nor creative ideas nor joy nor intellectual diversity nor allowance for dissenting opinion from subordinates.

Her administrators in the Green Valley Unified School District easily recognized one of their own, and she was soon chosen to be a candidate for principal, not by virtue of her teaching ability, which is never a reason one is picked for this weighty position, but by her eager adherence to the rules, no matter how skewed the rules were from the center of reason and logic, and common sense and decency. Her superiors would never promote to administrator a Teacher who had their own ideas about anything, for such Teachers would be considered dangerous, a movable cog in the wheel, liable to bring down the whole mechanism.

It is with the death of her third husband, ten years ago, that our story begins in earnest, for it is at this critical junction of her life where she gains a principalship, and when, for all intents and purposes, she becomes a general, a CEO, an executive, or, to be more exact, an Empress, and with Absolute Power over the lives of every person at her new school.

Beginnings

The school secretary at Amethyst Elementary, sitting behind the high-walled counter, was typing on the computer in the early a.m., when the first Teachers began to trickle in to the office.

"Good morning, Maria," each of them said to her, cheerfully.

Each time Maria heard a voice, she jumped out of her seat, for she expected the Principal to arrive at any moment.

"I'm taking command," a male voice sifted through the horrible striations of tension that crackled in the air; "it's a coup."

"Oh, James," Maria said, smiling largely, forgetting her woes for a moment, "you're in command, now? Is it a military or citizen coup?" She giggled for the sheer freedom of it.

James, aged twenty-nine, one year shy of the age he often said signaled the beginning of a human being's march toward death, feigned to go into the open doors of the Principal's office. "Raises for everyone," he said, grinning, "and, oh, it's a citizens' coup." He laughed as he looked upward, and then looked again toward Maria. "And now we have a four-day workweek. People are too serious around here."

"Oh, I like that, a four-day workweek; how marvelous," Maria gushed, beginning to forget her troubles.

"I have an idea," he said, turning toward the office door; "what if we put a detour sign right here," and he turned round with a wide smile of glee upon his youthful face, "which leads outside," and he walked, grinning still, to the two glass doors. He winked at the smiling secretary and opened one of the doors and pointed to the outside street, and said, "And we have signs going, well," and he pointed to the faraway green hills, "thataway." He danced over to the white-and-gray-speckled counter. "What say you, Maria? Do you think Margaret will fall for it?"

"Oh, I only hope she would," Maria replied, suddenly feeling depressed at the sound of her Mistress' name, and shaking her head, "but I just know she would not."

"Shoot," James returned, frowning. "I don't think she would, either. Hey," and he snapped his fingers as his swarthy face grew animated and then he skipped over to the office door again, "what if we walled up this area," and he massaged the air between the doorframes with care, "with concrete poured on it," he chuckled, "and we put boards on it that said 'Condemned.'"

"Before she comes or after she goes in?" Maria asked, merrily.

"Maria," James said, feigning displeasure, "I'm shocked that you would say such a thing."

"You know, I really can't stand her. She is so mean." The very speaking of it drove her near to tears.

James, abandoning his frivolous charade, walked solemnly up to the counter. "I know," he said, sadly, "of course, after she comes in." And a large, silly grin spread across his joyous face.

Maria laughed.

And then the voice of their taskmaster was heard ricocheting down the long corridor behind them like cannon fire, and the faces of the conspirators lost their festive mood.

James shook his head. "Something just blotted out the sun over this place," he said gravely, tapping gently on the ceramic top of the counter.

Mrs. Carbuncle, gray haired and wrinkle faced, walked in, her gait fast as she passed the circular counter. It shall be herein noted, at this particular moment, that she refused to have cosmetic surgery. She often said, regarding men and women in this matter, "Cut my face for men to lust after? I don't care what those brutes see in me, as long as it frightens them; and I don't give a hoot how women see me, either—the little bubbleheads don't interest me, except in their capacity as worker bees in my hive."

"Good morning," she sang, as if cheery.

"Good morning," Maria said, frowning.

James had already smartly vacated the premises.

Margaret was home now, in a place she mattered, where she was the final arbiter over the lives of thirty men and women who were college graduates and considered to be professionals. She could, with a glance, cause them to tremble or smile, to flee or embrace her. Power unfurled before her like a charging steamroller.

"I do love this job," she whispered to herself, clicking on her computer to check for emails from her Philosopher King, the Superintendent, from whom, as she saw it, all good things flowed. "Maria, would you come in here, please?" Her voice was soft and sweet, like the gentle humming of a hummingbird's colorful wings. Once Maria gave up the sanctuary of the outside—outside defined as not being inside the Principal's office—Margaret's voice assumed the rank of commander in the field of battle. "Maria, do you have those three parent letters I asked you to type? I'll be very disappointed if you do not." She was still looking at the computer screen, and when Maria began to impart excuses, her voice became like a sharp ax. "Well, stop whining and get on it; I don't pay you for standing around."

Maria walked to her desk, not wanting to cry, but her tears were on the way because she felt every verbal jab her tormentor thrust into her. Tears were the tiny messengers from her secretary's wounded heart, and Margaret understood this, and so she aimed them often and aimed them well at Maria to keep her subservient and afraid and respectful.

"Kindness on the job is a weakness," Margaret was fond of telling her youngest son. "People will only take advantage of you if you treat them civilly. And men, O, Roger, if you treat a man decently, he will sink his fangs into you and never let go." She had leaned closer to her small boy, resting her bony face upon his, and then whispered, her voice dark and menacing, "Men want to make me feel like a woman so they can dominate me...The monsters."

"Monsters," Roger had repeated, hating these faceless men as much as his beloved mother hated them.

After the bell rang to signal the students to assemble on the fading blacktop, Teachers led their students into the classrooms. Margaret waited, like a female leopard, watching the students disappear into the open doors; after a few minutes, her brown clipboard pressed between her flabby arms and brown-and-white-checkered dress, she moved out to what she perceived as her private hunting reserve.

The Law of Margaret Carbuncle

Margaret Carbuncle waltzed through each room of the school nearly every day simply to let the Teachers know it was she who held the reins of Power, that it was she who had the master key that opened any door. She moved with a quick, bent-over walk, her small, round head facing downward; her small eyes, like burnt wood in a pool of yellow quicksand, habitually darting about to discover some anomaly. She knew Teachers feared her unannounced entrances, and woe to those who were engaged in activities contrary to her personal prejudices.

She could walk through the room of a Teacher who was enlightened with the most recent research, a Teacher who could provide ample proof that their methods worked, and Margaret, the Empress of Amethyst Elementary, would simply ignore these facts if she disliked the Teacher. In such a classroom, Margaret saw only disharmony and bright, blinding colors and wild disorder that she could not distinguish from the sober, calm, comfortable world of lazy gray and fading white. Such a Teacher would catch her wrath with a poor evaluation, which might consist of a swipe of the truth mixed in with bald lies, or simply rambling, general statements that originated from Margaret's ignorance of what really was occurring in the classroom.

However, there were those few Teachers who, once absorbing Margaret's character and personality, could, in effect, do nothing but good. The Empress had to have those pious few who would be her loyal subjects and would worship her at all times.

What good is Absolute Power if there is not an audience to be in awe of it and adore it?

When Margaret C. Carbuncle saw her fanatical adherents in the light during those times, when this shining bright white light poured on all people and there was no reason for anyone to be devious and unkind and selfish—and indeed, even when her loyalists were not wicked at that time—she saw them in a particular brightness and color and degree of morality. When these same people were veiled in darkness, and their true natures were torn, with their own wicked teeth, from their false husk of flesh to expose their heinous and malevolent animal desires and deeds, Margaret saw them still in the same brightness and color and degree of morality. How could this be? And even when, as the light sprayed upon them, and these same people shed decency like a snake sheds skin, Margaret still saw them in the same flesh and tongue and mind and heart. How? It was because she and these people were of the same nature, as one.

Margaret had the singular ability to focus on a particular pattern in a person while ignoring the rest of the person, although it is true the pattern she concentrated on she skewed in her perverse mind.

One morning, Margaret walked into a room inhabited by a woman who was new to the district and had a secret she was anxious to divulge at the proper time to her Principal.

"Good morning, Mrs. Carbuncle," Yxta Beryl said, smiling radiantly, even though the eternal Game said to ignore the Principal in a classroom of students unless she acknowledged you first.

"Hello, Mrs. Beryl," Mrs. Carbuncle returned, smiling more at the district test scores, which were affixed with prominence to the stucco wall behind Yxta's richly flowing black hair.

In those Teachers who could coax high test results from their students, Mrs. Carbuncle found no ill thing—nearly.

"Why, I would pardon my mother's murderer if he could really teach," she often said to her precious boy, Roger, who, incidentally, often raised his crooked eyebrows at such eerie declarations.

Yxta made an error in judgment that day, even though in the end it did not matter. "Mrs. Carbuncle, you have been so busy lately I have not had the opportunity to tell you about my little miracle."

Mrs. Carbuncle put her right hand on Yxta's shoulder, a hand with its ornate jewelry and thick veins and black and blue marks creeping over it, and she turned her small head askew, looking for what she perceived was the object of the Teacher's affection. "Oh, the darling," she said, not really caring what child it was or caring who it was but that the child was bright and would contribute to high scores for the school.

"I'm pregnant, Mrs. Carbuncle," Yxta said, smiling, like a proud daughter speaking to her beloved grandmother; but at that exact moment, she felt the aged, wrinkled hand turn icy cold as it tightened its bony grip on her slender shoulder.

Margaret sought to smile, as was required of her station at this school while in the midst of Teachers and children, but she could not manage more than a creaky, lopsided one that seemed embedded in a thickening goo between horror and melancholy. "Why, isn't that wonderful," she managed to say, but she did not hear herself speak anymore, so full of rage was she. "Come by the office and tell me all about it at lunch," she finished, and she walked out of the door, never once acknowledging the greetings or the farewells of the students.

Lunchtime came and Yxta sat down on Mrs. Carbuncle's crimson-colored sofa, anticipating those requisite gifts of praise and congratulations from a woman she perceived as possessing maternal love and tenderness for her Teachers and students.

"We're not," Margaret began, "paying you good money to get pregnant. I just have to say how disappointed I am that you're pregnant now, of all times." Her wrinkled stare screwed up like crumpled paper as she shook her head. "This is a very selfish act."

Such language to Yxta was foreign, a language defined by a violent and abusive content directed at the recipient without just cause or remorse, and she was reluctant to interpret the substance of this attack as purely malevolent. She refused to believe any one particular person did not have some Goodness in them that could not be identified, cultured and grown so as to become palpable to any person looking for it. "Oh, Mrs. Carbuncle, I know this is a stressful time for you, but I know," and she smiled so warmly, as if indeed she was talking to a trusted friend, "you are happy for me."

"Children smell," Margaret growled, her thin lips palpitating, her small eyes, with their birdlike flitting, moving about in a frenzy. "You have an obligation to teach the entire year. This isn't a charity place. I don't want some incompetent substitute in your room." Her countenance became a grotesque, blood-red mask, like the color of smoke from an enormous fire that dined on living things. Her voice was flushed with an odious wrath that permeated and thickened the air. "You young women need to stop satisfying the lusts of men." She looked away in profound disgust. "Now, get out, you stupid girl."

Yxta was attempting to smile but the emptiness in her heart froze her face in shock. She would weep only a few minutes later at the idea that Mrs. Carbuncle was of a calm mind when she had uttered her smutty deprecation against her. "I just want to have a baby," she murmured in the quiet chambers of her classroom.

James, upon hearing Yxta's sobs through the thin wall that separated their rooms, was about to call out to her, but he abandoned the idea with the wave of his hand, and instead knocked on her door in the gentlest manner possible.

After Yxta invited him in, she told him what had occurred between her and Mrs. Carbuncle.

"She has extended her horizons in her hunger for persecution," he thought. "You'll be fine," he said smiling. "Don't let that 'germ' incarnate get to you. Or," and he feigned thoughtfulness, "is it 'bacterium'?"

Yxta laughed, drying her tears. "But she must have some decency in her; she has sons, and she taught for so many years…" In her voice was the search for some antecedent event in Margaret's life that could well define her cruel actions.

"I am just guessing now," James replied, amused, "but taskmasters who beat slaves probably have little affection for them."

"But she seems to be happy at our staff meetings," she remonstrated, diffidently.

In the marketplace of stylish acting with a designed purpose to deceive and numb an audience, no actress held greater acclaim in the hallowed annals of the theater than Margaret C. Carbuncle, for here, in the company of human beings, she could rewire their very brains and cleanse their minds of all distressing thoughts and doubts they had about her. Only the strongest Teachers, those who possessed a mind that ran on a different track, could put up a sufficient barrier to keep out her guileful and cunning ruses.

Meetings

"I just love children," Margaret said one fine day to her Teachers as she walked about the library; in fact, it was a sweet, aromatic Autumn day when the Summer heat has lain down its blazing sword and the Winter cold is still plotting how to torment the populace. She was prancing about like a little girl, gesticulating about and smiling. "Those little darlings just make my day—that's why I got into teaching, you know; they're just so lovable and eager to learn." Then she manufactured solemnity into her doughy, pasty face as she stood still and erect. "Woe to the Teacher who is here just for the paycheck, doesn't like children, bored by the job." She shook her head as she looked to the blue carpet, her wrinkled, old, brown-spotted hands held behind her soft, flabby back. "Can't have that," she said gravely, now waving her right hand about; "you won't last with Mrs. Carbuncle if you don't have a heart for these little children. Now, I'm not saying they're all perfect," she glanced up at her mesmerized audience, "but what I am saying is that you have to teach them like you would your own child. Do you," she frowned, "do you understand what I mean?"

What did all this mean? some of the Teachers mused, at least those who had previously decoded Margaret's strategic goals for the school; they pondered more questions: how could she mix such eloquent praise and apparent loyalty and love for children, while, in reality, be a cold, waxen figure whenever a child approached her? And was she not an unrelenting, grizzly, amoral assassin against those Teachers who spoke against her tyranny? And had she not hardened her heart toward those few who said nothing against her but were loathed by her simply for who they were or what they did?

James passed a note to Yxta that depicted their Principal's deformed head on both sides of the same coin. One side had "The Illusion of Goodness," written on it, while the other side had "The face of Evil is seen only by those who can truly see," written above the crudely drawn picture of a witch's head. James then carefully tucked the paper into his pocket.

Mrs. Carbuncle had begun the meeting at one o'clock in the p.m. on this minimum day for the school, and she deliberately kept the entire staff not only to the time when they could officially depart the campus, but long past it.

At a Principals' meeting the next day with her Superintendent, she boasted of her absolute domination over her Teachers.

"Those Teachers sit in staff meetings like rabbits caught in the glare of a trucker's headlights," she said, sneering. "Those fools believe whatever I tell them; why, they're like children."

"They are children," one of her male counterparts interjected, scowling.

She smiled in glee. "I purposely keep them in meetings past their contract time to leave, and they just sit there, scaredy-cats, every one of 'em." She giggled. "I violate the contract in a different way every week and still no one says anything; goodnight, were we so spineless, Daniel?"

The principal to her right was a man with slicked-back, brown, oily hair, and a bony, fleshy face that had the spider web lines and purple hue of the drunk, a man who wielded Power as freely as if it were merely another emotion to express. A black, enveloping disdain assembled itself across his arrogant face. "We are the ones with the backbone, Margaret; if they had a spine, they would be sitting next to us."

"What if they do begin to organize one day?" asked Edward, the newest principal, a young man of only thirty-three.

The Superintendent's baggy jowls shook, his large head bobbing about as he laughed uproariously. He did not have to speak to communicate his desires or knowledge of events right now; his silence implied it and his laughter spoke it. This was real Power.

"As long as you give the sheep lots of money," another principal said, frowning, "and not even what they deserve or what the district can give them, then they won't say a word even if we crucify one of their own right in front of them."

"We do that all the time as it is—crucify them," Margaret said, and it seemed as if she were growling, the same savage tone a harpooner makes when he teaches a fellow sailor how to thrust the dagger-tipped javelin into the innocent whale. "And the little fools bow their heads and run the other way every time."

"But doesn't anyone challenge us?" Edward asked, clearly bewildered, but wanting to believe in this dark magic.

It was time for the Superintendent to speak, and he passed his regal, fat, purple gaze at all of them, silencing them immediately, and then chose his words with great care, as does the artist in selecting the finest brush and the most exquisite colors for his painting. "Ladies and gentlemen," he began, slowly, as if the words that crawled out of his large mouth were more profound, "during the war, it was a mere handful of skinny little guards," and he held out his enormous, upturned hand, "who would keep hundreds of prisoners and the like from escaping from the camps. Yes, Edward," he said directly to the new Principal—he preferred to speak to all of his subordinates by their first names, "once in a while, one prisoner would try and escape and challenge the guards, and inevitably the misguided little fool would find himself married to a barbed-wire fence. No one," he said, again addressing all of his people, and then leaning closer to the center of the magenta-colored mahogany table at which they all sat, "is going to lead the charge of prisoners against the guards, because he knows if he looks back," he smiled, grimly, and then whispered, "his fellow prisoners will be running away." There, his canvas was now covered in masterfully bold strokes, and all his human appendages could do was behold its grandeur.

There was a requisite amount of silence that had to last for a long while to coat these words so they could be sealed on the minds and hearts of his loyal minions.

"People are like blades of grass," Margaret finally said, strumming the air with her sausage-like fingers, her eyes aglow with the luminous daggers of killing indiscriminately. "The first time you step on grass, it bounces back to its full height, but every time you step on it after that, the blades begin to weaken, until they wilt." She popped a pink pill into her quivering mouth. "And then one day, the grass is beaten down; and there you have it, you have a clear path, designed by your own will." She had been careful not to exceed the analogy of her executive and dull his sparkle.

"Utopia," Edward murmured, awestruck.

"Yes," Margaret said, screwing up her small, gray eyes and shooting their steely gaze into his youthful face, "Thomas More would be so proud."

"Well, no, he would not be," thought Edward, who fancied himself a philosopher, "but this is our Golden Age."

The Carbuncle Order of Things

Every workday was the same series of events for Margaret. She arose at six o'clock in the a.m., showered, and then drained a cup of strong black coffee while nibbling on a chocolate donut. She ate small meals because she knew that large meals would cause her to be sluggish. She drove her white Mercedes Benz to work, and like any good strategist in war, cogitated on the next battle. "I want my Teachers to breathe my morning exhalations," she was fond of saying to her own kind, "and that is why I must be there, if I can, before those sneaky creatures come in; but you can bet I won't leave until the last puckfist is gone. If I leave any of them alone for a moment, the pathetic idiots will rob me blind."

There was a prevailing theory among the Teachers that Mrs. Carbuncle would not leave campus until every Teacher had left the school. James was chosen by the Opposition Forces, which acted secretly on campus, to test this theory.

And so, every day for five days, James stayed until ten o'clock in the p.m., ensconced in his room, feigning to be toiling at projects when Carbuncle deliberately came by on what Teachers referred to as "snooping expeditions." She would peer anxiously through his window, or charge through his room, not saying a word, not looking at him, but merely plowing ahead, her face spastic with tics and grimaces as she streamed through. She, indeed, left later than he did the entire week.

But there would be a price to pay for James' bold venture. Immediately following this experiment, Margaret came to his room eight times in one month and issued to him the worst evaluations of the year.

"You are not surprised," Artemus said, sitting at his teacher's desk, looking up at his agitated pupil.

James shook his head. "I knew the job was dangerous when I took it."

Artemus laughed. "Quoting cartoon characters won't save you from Margaret."

"But I have documented everything she has done."

"Good," Artemus said, pleased that someone had listened to his sagacious advice on how to defend oneself against vindictive supervisors. He sat there with the casual air of intelligence whispering all about his kindly face. To hear him speak on any philosophical-, moral- or employment-related issue was to hear amiable and secretive whispers that danced mightily around his words. "Did we not tell you so?" echoed under and beside and inside his sagacious tones and intonations. "Is he not smarter than the rest of you, and even wiser than anyone else you can think of or pretend to know?" laughed and twinkled and finally lay, like the Cheshire cat, atop his salient and erudite speech. His answers were never rude, though he easily could have manipulated his carefully constructed sentences with a savory choice of "Don't you understand anything?" and "don't you ever listen?" Or he simply could have reached back and thrown some verbal hot spice and snickering black pepper at his befuddled audience and let his inflection and tone proclaim his intellectual talents over all of them.

Artemus and James conversed on the topic of Margaret's palpable and careless abuse of the laws and regulations to which the entire school district deferred.

"But she is violating so many education codes," James exclaimed. "Why hasn't she been challenged?"

"You're young, Jim," Artemus stated, in a manner that implied he knew where Jim had been, where he was, and where he was going. "People do not understand such esoteric matters, and even if it were explained to them, they would still not understand it. Look, it is like this," and his old and gentle countenance grew profound, "people simply do not act according to the dictates of common sense at every moment; people are irrational, illogical, emotional creatures who don't always do what they ought. Look," he said, frowning, "James, everyone knows you shouldn't smoke, drink to excess, eat unhealthy foods, ingest powerful, mind-altering drugs—well, nearly everyone—and conversely, that they should exercise, be kind and loving and faithful to their family and friends and spouse. Jim, for goodness' sake," he said, nearly laughing, "sin! Cheating, lying, adultery, murder, jealousy, violence—people aren't angels, they aren't terribly bright, but in the end, they nearly always do the right thing when they have their backs against the wall. But in this case, to challenge such established authority, I am afraid too many people say 'yes' externally but internally say 'no' to authority figures like the Margaret Carbuncles of the world. People are like pebbles swept down the stream, Jim, my boy, and for that pebble to turn and go upstream—why, that hurts, doesn't it, and now you no longer have the company of your fellow pebbles, nor their collective presence to deter the large ripples that normally befall them." He pursed his lips now, a signal that he was nearly finished with his soliloquy, and then he released them, cutting off James' impetus to reply. "In the end, though, people are just too busy to deal with people like Margaret Carbuncle. It's certainly easier to just let it go." There, he folded his muscular arms, pursed his thin lips, and leaned back, as if to say, "Now I am completely done, and you may state your reply—and please, take as long as you wish."

Jim sat down. "But it isn't right, the way we're treated." He shook his head, thinking of Yxta. "You seem so relaxed."

"Well," he returned, quickly, "that's because I'm not here most of the time." He smiled at Jim's bewildered look. "You see," he said, closing his luminous, brown eyes, "I only came back right now to speak to you."

"What?" Jim cried, unable to suppress his exclamation of surprise.

Artemus spoke in a clear, concise manner, the words trickling out of his mouth with ease. "You see, Jim, after you leave this room, I will go back to my very private high mountains with my very private pristine lakes where the warm sun caresses my face," and for a moment his mature visage changed, nearly imperceptibly, as he looked past his audience. In a moment, the eerie expression of indifference evaporated. "We will talk, later; if I talk too much now, I will lose the day; and oh, Jim, if you were like me, and you will be soon enough, you would not want to lose one precious moment of Paradise."

Indeed, in just a few seconds after his last words, Artemus, elderly and white haired, appeared not to remember the conversation he had just had with his passionate apprentice. Later that night, at Artemus' home, while his wife read a book on philosophy in her room, he revealed his fantastic Secret to James.

"It is the Secret of the Ages," James murmured, dumbfounded, "but you must tell the world."

"Ah," Artemus replied, his arms folded in his checkered, multicolored plaid shirt as he rested comfortably on his sofa, "but no one would listen."

"May I tell them?" asked the eager youth.

Artemus laughed. "Yes, but I warn you," he said, and suddenly he grew solemn, and his words bore an augury of doom, "you will only be disappointed in them."

A Year In

The school year ended for Amethyst Elementary School and the Teachers felt as if their skin had been lacquered in a venomous ooze mixed with a tawdry, rancid spit that could only be peeled away through distance and time from the place.

Mrs. Carbuncle had marked her first year as Principal here in the same manner as animals releasing their phero- mones in the wild to mark their territory. Margaret did it through personally engaging people in small, close encoun- ters, where she opened her wide, multi-fanged mouth and clamped tight onto their heads and gnawed away at their naked emotions until their minds felt the gash deep with- in their fractured, protected borders. From her yawning yel- low mouth squeezed the black drops of her poison, which dripped onto the tender skin of her hapless victims. Those who had the bite of this vampyra were easily distinguished from those without her signature mark upon them, for those marked walked like the undead: tilted, withered, their energies exhausted, their enthusiasm smothered, their eyes hollowed out so that only a dull, lusterless gloom survived within.

And those whom Margaret favored, those who were informants for her, why, they huddled tightly against each other under her black, icy shadow for protection, and for nourishment they sucked a numbing narcotic from her crusty, sagging old breasts, letting the slimy, gray milk of bitterness and pettiness flow into their yearning mouths; malice and an undiluted, purposeful arrogance coursed through the cor- roded arteries of the Ice Queen's adherents, and their small, cold hearts pumped this cruel juice to feed itself and become thick and hard and sooty as it mixed with the ashen vapor of its victims.

Those whom Margaret slew with her icy, rabid breath, she persecuted without cause and kept most of them at her school because she simply enjoyed grinding down the will of those she perceived as weak, and also to show her supe- riors she would keep all of her little scared chickens in one big coop; but, more importantly, she kept nearly all of the

Teachers at Amethyst Elementary whether they were silent or aggressive against her because, ultimately, they did not fight back. "In their minds they slay dragons, and they fight me," she often boasted to the Teachers she had brought with her from her other school, where she had been Principal for fifteen years. "Ha! One day, even they will acquiesce to my every whim."

Throughout the year, she perfected techniques that involved purifying her assaults upon the Teachers' neurotic psyches.

She could appear in a classroom without anyone recalling her entrance, just as if she were indeed a vampire who had transformed itself into a cold, black mist that had crawled underneath the heavy green door. Holding her black, hard plastic clipboard with pink evaluation forms on it—some forms nearly completed before she had entered her victim's room—she would cast her ghoulish glance about the room as the students and Teacher nearly jumped out of their tingling skin. If the Teacher in that particular classroom was doing anything Margaret deemed suspicious, such as students learning about life or history or science or anything that was not to be found on the annual state tests, why, she would sit down and write as many falsehoods as she could possibly cram onto the sheet; if, however, the Teacher was performing their duties accordingly, then, depending on Margaret's temper, but more often than not, she exited the room without writing anything. Yet, she would leave slowly, with a knowing scowl that indeed she might return at any given moment. It was Margaret's plan to walk in on lessons that had a greater chance of being interpreted on her evaluations as dysfunctional and incompetent. "Why," she often said at her Principals' meetings, "the fools never rebut the overt lies I put on those evaluation forms—they sicken me!" Her thin lips would keep palpitating after this, as if they were not finished with their ridicule of the Teachers. "One or two of the idiots sometimes grumble or gripe, but one look from this old, gray-haired woman—boo!" she would cry with delight, giggling like a high priestess stirring a cauldron of steaming potions, "and they back down like whipped dogs." And then she would grin and scrunch up her small, sharp nose. "I would hate them less if they showed some old-fashioned guts." She turned her birdlike, blinking eyes and bobbing head round the room to glance at her peers. "Of course, I would still break their will like you do to any trained dog."

Everyone howled.

The second school year began, and James and Maria, in the office the day before classes began, were talking about those few Teachers who had been transferred.

"But Harriet and Martin weren't a threat to Margaret," Maria stated, innocently, nearly crying for people she had known for so long.

James smiled a sad, despairing smile that wept for old friends missed. "They had the misfortune of having a disproportionate amount of students in their rooms who weren't too terribly bright."

"Oh, my goodness; low test scores."

The easy demeanor he had possessed since childhood, a translucent, inner philosophy that had served him best in love and war and kept his inner pipes and pumps free of clogs and wear and tear, began to dissemble before her; it was a transposition of ideas and circumstances previously shunned from his inner psyche that Maria saw assemble in rank and file upon his sad visage; she could see that his posture had drooped, his arms dropped to his sides, his deep, brown eyes were bleeding pathos. "Maria, Maria," he began, his voice covered in grief, "we are the hunted; Teachers are hunted, we

are—they wage an open persecution against us, just as the
Jews in Europe were persecuted and blamed for every blemish
and sin, just as the man with black skin was once persecuted
and blamed for every blemish and sin in the South; O, they
stand boldly and accuse us, without shame…" but he shook
his head and looked about the place that he knew should be
a refuge from the influences of sinister forces, and he sighed.
Maria dared not move, for fear of impeding the pain that
needed to fall from his lips. "You know what the legislators
did, they went ahead and did it, didn't they, Maria; they gave
us that piece of legislation that made test scores into everything, and made Teachers accountable for everything, too;
so now, we are the hunted, they—and I mean lawmakers
and newspapermen and businessmen and anyone else who
opens wide their ignorance—they seek us everywhere, they
accuse us, they taunt us, they rail against us, and they chase
us down—like cowards, they hide in newspaper articles, on
talk shows, in mobs, who do their bidding; why, we are on
the bottom rung of society, above criminals, below even animals—why, Maria, even animals have more rights than us,
and dead animals, too! And you want to know the worst of
it—we have no champion! No one will stand with us or in
front of us—no one, and so we are finally alone." There, she
saw it, there was a trace spark of illumination in his eyes for a
moment, and then it died, horribly, snuffed out by the bitter
reality of his words. "And do you know what else it has done,
Maria, do you know? Why, it has allowed avaricious principals and superintendents to sprout up everywhere—like fun-
gus—sticking their slimy roots into our schools and sucking
us dry as they grow fat on our labor—and they work us like
dumb oxen, too; and oh, they beat us like slaves, and they
want us to make bricks without straw, and do you know what
we do, Maria, do you know what Teachers do? Why, we take

it, we take it and we take it and take it, until finally we can't take it anymore." But his core being of frivolity and joy would not allow him to trespass too long into this dark territory of lamentation. "But we're in the middle of it now, Maria, we are, but you know what," he said, suddenly snapping his fingers and quickly nodding his head and standing taller, and as he did so, Maria, as if attuned to his inner rhythms and melodies, sat up too and spread a felicitous smile across her swarthy countenance, "we will outlast them all, because we always outlast them, Maria, we do; and do you know why, Maria?" And, there it was, that large, shining grin of his that could subdue any sober and sour mood. "Because we are bigger than all of them, that is why," and he laughed, he truly laughed and his mouth was open wide and his eyes sparkled as he raised his arms above his head in a victory salute; "just let them come and get us! Let them come—hey!" he laughed, gesturing defiantly. "Soon they'll have our pictures on 'wanted' posters," and he framed the air with his hands as Maria laughed heartily, "dead or alive—yes, dead or alive for this Teacher—and why?" and he paused for effect, suppressing his mirth, "Low test scores!"

Maria applauded and smiled and laughed as he took a bow, and then she said, thoughtfully, "James, you really should write an article to the newspaper about this."

He bowed gracefully, and then said, with a sly grin, "Maybe I will!"

But then his voice sank into the abyss that was littered with the crowded tombs of Teachers' careers, for he saw Maria's grim face. "Yxta," he murmured, and turned so as not to weep, "I pray for Yxta not to come back."

Maria put her old hand upon his shoulder. "You know she has to, James. You know they froze her out after giving her that unsatisfactory evaluation, by refusing to give her letters of recommendation. She has nowhere else to go. This is her family."

"O Maria, Yxta's baby; O Maria, not Yxta, all she wanted was a baby."

"She is a fighter, Jim, you know that; she won't allow them to bully her."

James, to usurp this melancholy scene, walked to Margaret's door and thrust his arms out toward it. "What if I put a 'For Sale' sign across it? Do you think she will figure it out?"

"No," Maria replied, laughing, and slapping her hands together on high, "she would just pull it down with her bad attitude."

"How about if I have her office removed," his face grew animated, "and wheeled away," he paused, rubbing his chin, "to Siberia?"

"We can't do that to our Russian friends. Do you want the Cold War back?"

"Maria!" James exclaimed. "You're becoming a regular comedian."

The prattling voice of their Mistress shattered their festive mood, and James departed, but whispered on his way out, "Thank you for being our point woman."

Maria smiled and whispered to him, but then Margaret came in like an icebreaker ship.

"Why are you standing around—get to work!" she snapped, feigning anger, and then smiled as she disappeared into her office. She was home.

Maria felt as if covered in an oozing, degenerate slime. "Is there no justice?" she mused.

Saffron

Our story would not be complete without including Saffron Willow, a woman of African and Native American descent, a woman who became a Teacher because she thought with her Heart and Mind and Spirit. It was her Heart, primarily, that led her to deliver children to the high vault of learning, but then her Mind decided that more good things could be done for children if she were an administrator, and so she completed her administrator's credential and became an Assistant Principal during the last school year.

She had now been at Amethyst Elementary School for ten years.

During her first year with Margaret C. Carbuncle, she felt her morals erode fiber by fiber as her resistance to the tyranny of Absolute Power weakened, and this Power was slowly and meticulously absorbed into her, its viral self invading her cell by cell and replicating itself in her and replacing her benign self with its malignant being. Each day, the march of this tiny, resilient virus and its savage brethren, Lust, Jealousy and Love of Self, echoed down the many dark corridors to her heart, slippery pathways that were newly scratched and gouged; crooked, lumpy roads that were built when she willingly took up residence in the dark tower of undiluted absolutism.

During the early days of the new school year of the second-year reign of Margaret, Saffron sat in Margaret's office, listening to her supervisor plot out the next nine months in intricate detail.

The first days of the school year are like the first hours of an infant's birth, every moment being precious and crucial to its successful growth, and Margaret had long ago decided she would personally hard-wire the brain of her baby and be its sole source of nourishment.

"These Teachers are lazy by nature," Margaret said, scrunching up her sharp nose while her head peeped around the edge of her desk, her squinty eyes looking out into the office, "and they're inherently sneaky people." Margaret thought that anyone who did not palpably disagree with her about such issues must agree with her, and therefore, must be like her; which is to say, that such a person is no longer a Teacher, having passed into the upper echelon where the gods of business dwell and watch closely over the lives of the ignorant peasants. "This year we're going to separate the wheat from the chaff, if you get my drift," Margaret continued, a smile beginning but dying upon her frozen visage, because smiles of joy for the sake of others were unable to take root upon the sterile soil of her stone face, and because joy for herself was actually a frightening kind of amalgam of a stretched, bushy scowl and a wicked, creeping laugh. Her own smiles were planted in small cavities of fertilizer on her ashen face, a black, mushy manure composed of tiny bits of epidermis collected every time she stealthily crept up behind an educator to catch them in a bad moment of teaching. And O, how the minute flakes of skin cells of the Teacher would float all about and trickle down like a sudden snowstorm at such times!

Every moment Saffron sat in this office, with its maroon oak desk and the computer and copier and the plaques of degrees and awards on the wall, she was being impregnated by Margaret with the seeds of arrogance, and as it arose in Saffron, it coincided with a decline in her capacity for Justice and Compassion and Kindness.

Margaret could feel the specific aroma-coded-germs-of-Power slowly envelop her young assistant, and she could see the silky lace of conceit and condescension drape over the woman, and she was pleased. "You're one of us, now," she confessed to herself at that moment, "and you shall live in the nebula of true Power on Earth, where the subjugation of others who willingly accept all kinds of abuse is freely given to you."

"Why, you have been chosen, Saffron, with great care," she whispered, and then she dropped her head and her high-pitched voice, almost as if she were angry. "Don't you believe it was a mistake; those fools out there," and she disregarded the Teachers not only at her school but everywhere with a quick motion of her jewelry-laden hand, "couldn't do what we do; no sir, they don't have the stomach for it; you know what Mrs. Carbuncle calls 'em? Pill bug people, that's what they are," and she motioned with her right hand a small circle; "they just close up into tiny balls and roll away into the corner and tremble when I walk by; that's who they are and who we are not, not a bit." She patted her blue blouse on her flabby stomach, and then tapped her bony, white skull. "They don't have the brains, either—when you're as old as I am, you realize some people are born to rule and others to serve." She seemed thoughtful as she screwed up her eyes and pursed her thin, dry lips. "It isn't whether it's right or wrong, dear, it's just the way it is." She reached out and touched Saffron, and her voice seemed wrapped in a gauzy web of prophecy. "It's who you are, and you can't change it; why," and she leaned back, her wizened face animated, "since time immemorial, people have been struggling to conquer each other and live in peace." An opening of bewilderment spun wider and wider in her visage until its magnificent hyperbole engulfed her entire wriggling body. "The answer is here, don't you see it? We're it," she exclaimed, with authority, expecting her apprentice to embrace this revelation, "it's business, it centers everything; no need for wars, now; heck, just let the businesses and their leaders, like you and I, run things, and let the rest of the world work for people like us and it would be just fine." She nearly smiled. "I truly believe that one day the entire world will be composed of millions," and she squealed out that last word, "of businesses employing everybody, making everybody happy. Those fools out there need us or they'd starve to death—and Teachers? Bah!" she said, exasperated, knocking down their image with a slap of her hand to her skinny thigh, "they're nothing but peasants who can read and pass tests; not one of them could do what we do, and if they could, they would."

Saffron grew another layer of self-righteousness that day.

Yxta

Yxta walked into her room, F25, enthusiastic for the success of her students, an attitude she carried with her every morning, a sublime passion which desired that even her most emotionally troubled students would begin to respond to her guidance.

Her fifth-grade classroom was decorated with the highest hopes of free and unconditional optimism; it was infused in every one of her thousand books in the ten brown bookcases; it hung on the classic works of art, dwelt on the glossy History and Science and Civil Rights posters; it radiated from the brightly multicolored walls that contained her students' work. Hope beamed from the special posters that sang of Love and Respect and Justice for all, and pride emanated from posters that whispered of self-esteem and confidence in oneself.

The refulgent soul of this room was Knowledge and Learning, which lead to empowering oneself so a person might have every opportunity to succeed in life.

Mrs. Carbuncle would walk into classrooms at specific times when she supposed that her hunted game might be having difficulty with control of their environment, and this meant those chaotic moments before recesses and after recesses and after physical education and after lunch. In the event that chaos did not prevail in a classroom, then she had a remedy for that, too.

One fine Autumn day, when the hot, yellow sun caresses the skin in a bubbly bath of warm kisses, and the gentle breezes clear the air of all kinds of unpleasant smells, there was a panoramic, deep, smoky cerulean expanse of rich, clean sky, and all who saw it expressed a sincere gratitude to simply stand under this prismatic treasure. It was on this glorious day that Mrs. Carbuncle walked into room number F25, carrying in her head an exact set of parameters with which to evaluate her quarry. Looking up at the august sky before she entered, she saw nothing of its natural beauty, only its endless oceans and a seemingly endless boundary. "There are my limits." She smiled, and she walked in through the back door of the room to appear inside it as if she had indeed arisen through the aquamarine carpet. A healthy grimace, dripping with a terrible, aching want, lived in the doughy complexion of her pitted and creased old face; her lips began to palpitate when she soon realized that no chaos was to be found here, and her small, round head with the curly gray bun atop it bent down with its two sinister eyes sunk deep within its skulking face.

Her two gray orbs were like the chewed pits from the fruits of temptation; these eyes, these festering rings of fiery bitterness, had been pushed in so deep by the forces of darkness that they now cloaked their true nature from the world of Good Men.

Mrs. Carbuncle sat down and steadily and ferociously commenced writing every foul and treacherous lie she could burn in calories during her one half-hour stay.

After watching Mrs. Carbuncle exit out the front glass door—this Principal who never once acknowledged the students in this room—Yxta walked over to her own desk to pick up the pink copy of the evaluation form. Her heart pounded in expectation as she silently read it. The libelous nature of the document colored the air in a sooty, oily haze and poisoned the room with its enthusiastic, uninhibited lies. "Let me read to you what our Principal observed," she said, vexed beyond reason, but composing her emotions sufficiently to deliver the false words of her oppressor. "'Few of the students are paying attention. Five students are coloring. Three students have their feet on their desks. The students seemed bored.'"

One of her more aggressive students, who would one day begin an authentic third political party in America, shouted, full of rancor, "The woman is a wretch!" He would one day cite Yxta as one of the most important influences in his life.

"Yeah," the chorus from his comrades echoed, though they had no idea what "wretch" meant.

Yxta smiled, proud of their loyalty, exhaled in a long expulsion, and then continued, now walking about the room. "'The Teacher seemed confused about the direction of the lesson, confusing the students.'"

"What room was that old bat in?" one of her male students cried, outrage puckering his face into an incredulous frown.

"She was in the nuthouse in her nutty head," a female student added, with great passion, happy to attack unkind women who were in positions of power, something that came from the deepest depths of her young female heart.

The fifth-grade students laughed as does a group that imagines their tormentor in pain.

After the day was over, Yxta carefully videotaped her room, and secured the students' work in a manila envelope, all of which could be used as evidence against her persecutor.

The inner dynamics of Amethyst Elementary for the Teachers became survival, and this meant to appease the ogre when necessary, and although this was important, it was also necessary to avoid the monster at all other times.

"Of course, it is best to stray completely from the main office, thus reducing your chances of being found out and being asked questions she would otherwise have forgotten in another minute," James said to a young female Teacher whom he considered his apprentice. He smiled. "I can see you need a personally guided tour on playing the Game; well," and he extended his bent arm for her to grasp, "step this way, mademoiselle."

Entering the lounge at lunchtime, James and his companion, Celeste, were encased in a protective shell spun by James' careful and specific instructions, which were, simply stated, "Watch, listen, say nothing, and learn."

Thus removed from the frenetic interaction radiating from the core of Teachers, they settled in the corner of the small lounge area on a tan sofa and observed the shifting conversations in this small community.

The females talked about their children, their husbands, their aches and pains, their moods and their weight; the men spoke of family matters, sports, wives, children, and political matters; but very few of them spoke of their problems concerning students.

One of the women mentioned Margaret Carbuncle, and the Teachers around her stopped their conversations to listen, for they had long ago decided that their Principal was the nucleus of the school's multitude of problems.

"She wouldn't suspend Gregory," she moaned, massaging her aching, chubby feet. "This morning, at recess, he kicked Alice, the Yard Duty Supervisor, and after Alice brought him up to her, she told Alice to get out of her face and quit bothering her." She watched the faces of her listeners drop into the brown mire of disbelief. "She told Alice to give Gregory more space on the playground, and so now he runs around and does whatever he wants. And how do I know she said all of this? I was there," she groaned emphatically, waving her finger about, "I heard it all."

"And Margaret boasts at meetings that she suspends fewer students than other schools because of our counseling methods," a male Teacher said, disgusted.

Of course, not to laugh meant you weren't listening, so everyone who was listening had to laugh—no, wanted to laugh at the absurdity of it all, and specifically at this upside-down world Margaret Carbuncle had created, where she lived by the motto "There is no such thing as bad students, only bad Teachers."

One of Margaret's compatriots walked in, and James nudged Celeste's arm, nodding his head to the coming reaction one could hear and see only if one was a strict adherent to the agreed-upon rules while playing the all-important Game.

The woman who had initiated the conversation with her remarks about her troubled student said, "And then one of my other students," and she was certain to say it in the direction of the Mole who had just walked in, "was trying to eat a sandwich that was in his desk, and every time he reared up his head, he had mustard all over his face. And of course, he denied it; and oh, I found an open Coke can in his pocket, too."

Again, everyone laughed, a hearty laughter directed at the Informant who was getting a cold beverage from the soft drink machine, a laughter that spoke a special language to her unconscious mind, "Do you hear us? No reason to repeat our trivial conversation to our boss, right? We weren't talking about your friends, understand? We're just letting out a small geyser of steam so we can finish the day without losing control of our emotions."

But the female Teacher who had spoken about her student had made a critical mistake in admitting, even in a humorous manner, that there were discipline problems in her classroom. The next morning, the secretary called the Teacher in her classroom to tell her the Principal wanted to meet with the Teacher after school. The message had been delivered early in the day so the woman could suffer to the greatest depths of her imaginings. The poor female Teacher had not yet learned to play the coveted Game at the highest level of expert.

Yxta Comes Alive

The human mind can hold only so much anti-joy matter before it automatically shuts down for repair. There are safety valves inherent in the complex wiring of the brain network, and before a maximum level of anti-joy matter clogs up this spongy, gray matter, the brain will make adjustments in the most curious ways.

The Game continued.

At a staff meeting that same day, James sat comfortably between Yxta and Celeste, passing secret notes back and forth to his two charming allies.

"I just love children," Margaret began, smiling as she pushed out her sagging, wrinkled-looking chin. Her eyes squinted when she giggled, "I just love the little ones, they're so cute. When I hear that someone is pregnant I just get goose bumps. Lynn is pregnant. Isn't that wonderful news?" Lynn was a first-class snitch, blabbermouth and exquisite squealer who somehow had not bypassed the adolescent stage of tattle-telling.

Lynn was the ultra-patriot kind of super rat who would sell her baby for a quarter if Margaret needed the money for a phone call.

Of course, Lynn had asked permission of her mentor-goddess-matriarch if she might get pregnant and have the baby. "Right when Summer begins; and then right when Summer ends, it goes to day care," Margaret had said after sulking and cogitating for months on the idea of her acquaintance desiring pregnancy; and she had only assented to this request because she had decided that Lynn would serve her even better if she, Margaret, allowed Lynn to conceive.

"The fools at work will think I love babies," Margaret had said to herself after this decision. "Babies smell. Ugh."

As Margaret waltzed over to rub Lynn's shoulders, Yxta sat, stone-faced, staring with cloaked venom in her eyes that smoldered from an eternal fire deep within her vermilion hues, a fire with roots deep within the psyches of those unjustly persecuted, a fire that burned clean and waxed argent bright. This fire was unknown to those folks who have not been terrorized from within and without, and who have not lost their baby who dwelt inside them. From whence does this fire come? It came from Yxta's every waking breath and blinking eyes and emphatic thoughts that could see only one egregious image within its boundless horizons, and that was the agonizingly slow, torturous death of her tormentor. Right now, right there in the library, Yxta could feel her baby—whom, she reasoned, Margaret had murdered—right there in her own arms; she could feel the baby's soft, warm body against her body, and in her mind she looked down at the innocent child and saw this precious and innocent face look up at her. Yxta cried within the confines of her feminine heart, wherein her vengeance dwelt in an insatiable hunger, waiting for Justice to arrive.

Her reverie was interrupted by her nemesis moving about the place, working the Teachers much as a wolf in the guise of a sheep minds the flock. Margaret would bounce from topic to topic with the same logic a twister follows when it changes directions, but she was a human twister that would inflict damage on only those objects that did not bow down to it in public and pay homage to it.

Margaret's topics ranged from amusing anecdotes about her life to self-deprecating blurbs about herself and then to more sober matters, and then around and back to more incessant tidbits about anything and anybody—and for any reason; but more importantly, and tacitly, it was a searching expedition to see how her employees would respond to what she perceived as words of wisdom, but what the majority of Teachers perceived as blithering, blathering buckets of banal boasting and preposterous posturing.

Yes, there were a few Teachers who laughed very loudly, as if to say, "Look at me, I'm laughing at your humor!" And yes, there were also those who echoed her dramatic utterances, "...must educate all of the students" and "...raise those test scores."

Jim passed a note, clandestinely wrapped, to Yxta. It depicted a subterranean resort where the forces of darkness indwelt with their chosen prince; but the prince, smiling demurely, stood poised over a chair upon which sat Margaret, and, serving her tea, he said, "For you, Mother dear."

Yxta laughed inside of herself with such hilarity that James could see the fury of contempt in her eyes diminish; yet externally, she retained the same harsh grimace, accompanied by a cluster of frowns and looks of indifference.

After the meeting, Yxta was summoned by Mrs. Carbuncle to her office. "Congratulations again, Lynn," Margaret said to her fellow conspirator as she entered her office, smiling, making sure that she was always pleasant to those Teachers still in the outer shell of her office. The moment she shut the door and sat down at her maple desk, her countenance became savage, drained of all compassion. "You will not mock me at staff meetings, do you hear me?" she said, her voice growing with wrath as she stared at Yxta, who sat across from her. "You will not be allowed to frown and roll your eyes at my meetings. I will not have it." She went on and on and again and around the same topic she impaled with her fanatical desire for control.

"Is this a reprimand?" Yxta said, coolly, her face as smooth as the gravestone of her dead baby. "Are you going to write a written reprimand?"

Mrs. Carbuncle summoned in Saffron, who came in willingly. "You saw her frowning," Mrs. Carbuncle said to

Saffron, "you've had Teachers complaining about her negative attitude, haven't you?"

Yxta looked, with condemnation, at Saffron, who had to assent to her superior's query. "Name those Teachers," Yxta said, and then looked back to Mrs. Carbuncle. "Go ahead and write me up right now so I can show this to my lawyer that you are attempting to control my facial features. And I want union representation right now or I walk."

Mrs. Carbuncle's lips were throbbing like a madman's. Her small, round head was twisting about while her small, ashen-gray eyes looked all about the room. "You will not," she said, her face crunched in a sour clamp, "frown anymore at my meetings."

Yxta made a mistake then, but she wanted to test Mrs. Carbuncle. "I guess I have quite a bit on my mind."

Mrs. Carbuncle nearly rose out of her seat, outrage propelling her upward like a rocket. "You will not think about personal problems on my time—now, get out of here!"

After Yxta left, Margaret continued on. "Do you know why," Margaret began, screeching, while looking at Saffron, "Romans would crucify political prisoners along the roadside?" She stood up, and now her full fury was unleashed—there were no checks, no restraints or humanity left now in her crimson pool of madness—for she had come to accept Saffron as one who could see her, Margaret, for what and who she truly was, and like it. "They pounded nails into their bodies and let them hang there as an example to the rest of the Roman world." Her wizened face lit up with the fire of a breathing, living vengeance creeping toward her wicked bosom. "Beware, Yxta, beware!"

Saffron Ebbs and Flows

Saffron could feel her innate humanity ebb away each day while in the iron grip of Margaret C. Carbuncle; and as for the humanity she had acquired bit by bit—for each good deed and kind thought she had had her entire life, and for every lie she did not make or every time she did not gain through deception what others had lost through innocence, she felt this inner protective shell of layers beginning to crack.

"Well, she must have some good in her," Saffron recited to herself daily, and daily, she sought to find this elusive morality in her Supervisor. One day, after tiring of waiting to find Mrs. Carbuncle in a joyous mood, she decided to test her.

"Oh, Mrs. Carbuncle," she began, smiling, once the morning bell had rung and all of the classrooms were full, "I want to make this chicken dinner…"

"Eh? Chicken dinner? What's that?" Mrs. Carbuncle returned, her face screwed up in a quizzical frown, shaking her head as if to loosen these meaningless words from her big, drooping, earring-laden ears, and then, pushing away the remaining fragments of the words that still dangled about her, she whined, "I don't give a fig about chicken dinners, we have the School Site Plan to work on."

Saffron smiled because if she did not smile, she would have let loose the most horrible look of bewilderment.

But isn't this one of the things that women do best, to mask their bitter disappointments and pain with a pleasant smile?

However, there were ample times when Saffron observed Margaret proffer niceties to people, but mostly, these niceties were confined to Margaret's one son who could not function in society without the guidance of his mother, and for her granddaughters, on whom she lavished fine gifts and praise but very little of her own precious time.

"But how can she be so bad," Saffron said one day to her husband, who really wasn't paying attention but was putting on the façade of this necessary act as he secretly listened to the sports announcer call the basketball game on the radio. "Mrs. Carbuncle just dotes on her grandchildren." Saffron had to dress Margaret in at least a partly recognizable human skin so she, Saffron, could exist at her work without too much emotional strain. "I know she is a good woman; she just has so much pressure."

"Right," her husband said, frowning, because his other level of consciousness, developed exclusively during his early formative years as a faithful husband, had processed this particular tone of his wife's as one that required from him an affirmative, agreeable response. Yet, he managed to pull himself out of his sacred union with sports to utter a most curious remark, to which his dumbfounded wife could not respond. "Do not even sinners do good to those who do good to them?"

A human being moves from one country to another and absorbs the new culture and customs and foods because that is how people survive, by adapting to their new surroundings. Soon, that young person may have a thick, heavy accent, just as an indigenous citizen does. The new arrival does not step back and watch the accent develop, for it simply comes, just as language comes to an infant.

Saffron was now too tight inside Margaret's orbit to escape her gravitational pull, an object much bigger than Saffron, a force called Power.

It is true there is a select group of people who can resist the collapse of their own will into the mighty black blade of

Power, and they are called the Mavericks, but their singular breed is not understood by the general public, and the Mavericks are, ironically, often persecuted by those ordinary citizens who could most benefit from them.

Of course, Artemus was one of the Mavericks, and he had long ago deciphered one of the great secrets of the wise men, and it was this:

If a human being with a lucid mind and a burning desire for knowledge encounters any single Thing that does not appear to be what it is, and he desires to know its true identity, he must abate all of his previous endeavors and concentrate on that specific Thing, and in due time, the illusion of the Thing will disappear and reveal its True Nature to him; this, Artemus had done in no little time when he had encountered his first principal, and he had done it for every succeeding one since.

Before we turn to his story, however, let us interject a bit of levity into this bleak tale.

The Pink Boxes

Teachers of children in elementary schools are a breed set apart by their ability to deprive themselves of achieving many of their own goals in life, for the job of Teacher becomes a Holy Mission once they understand that the future lives of human beings are in their very hands.

The lounge of any school is the place where Teachers share their adventures with their colleagues, although the Teachers at Amethyst Elementary had to be careful not to divulge potentially damaging secrets to those certain few they had deemed "Margaret's Spies," or "MSs."

James and Yxta were talking of his recent impaling by Mrs. Carbuncle's evaluations. "As there are only three males left at this site, she must," James said, looking about as if he expected to see an intruder, "persecute those males left; why, today, she," his transition to another altogether different topic was seamless after he saw Them coming, "and did you know that the state budget for next year will allow for even more money for the schools?"

"Great," Yxta said, feigning joy as she too spied three of the MSs sisters coming through the door of the lounge. She giggled with glee when she thought of the ease with which this conversation had shifted to clear the air of any rotting debris left after smoking Mrs. Carbuncle's image to smoldering bits. She watched as James continued on, and as the MSs took their lunches from the refrigerator.

"They come late and leave early every day, and are often absent," Yxta said, after the spies had left. "They bother me. I know gossip is awful, but those women take advantage."

"Rumor has it that they aren't even marked absent on the payroll roster when they miss work."

Yxta's comely visage became indignant. "I think they need to acquire the 'pink boxes syndrome.'"

"Yxta!" James exclaimed, laughing.

While it is true that Teachers often deny themselves life's bigger pleasures throughout their careers, they do not deny themselves those smaller joys they feel are due to themselves, and in the case of food, those pleasures are the feeding on of sweets and fatty substances that are continuously in the lounge room. Whether there was one package of delectable bear claws or five bags of fudge cookies or home-baked cinnamon rolls on the table in the morning, all of these delicious snacks would normally be consumed by the Teachers before the sun rose to its zenith.

Putting a box of cookies in a Teachers' lounge is like placing a cup of white granulated sugar next to an anthill.

Was it someone's birthday? Creamy, frosted, savory cakes were brought into the lounge. Was it a baby shower? Female Teachers would stay up all night to bake sugary brown-rim cookies or chewy chocolate chips or fresh blueberry pies to bring to the blessed affair.

It is said, "Any excuse will serve a sweet tooth."

The pink boxes were the most ubiquitous item to be found in this employees' lounge, for they contained the elixir of life for frustrated, irritable workers.

"Donuts," Yxta whispered to James. "It's time we put some solid pounds on those man slaughterers, the MSs."

James laughed approvingly.

"After we get done with them, they'll be able to audition for the coveted role of the clown in the circus," and here she worked up a most vicious sneer, "but they won't even need the clown clothes."

The rest of the staff, already united against Carbuncle and the MSs, swore off the rich delights of the pink boxes.

The first week, two pink boxes appeared on a Friday in the lounge, and as usual, each box contained a dozen glazed and a dozen chocolate donuts, and all of them were subsequently devoured by the end of the workday by Carbuncle and the MSs.

The second week, four pink boxes appeared on the brown tables in the lounge, again on Friday, and once again, all of the succulent donuts were eaten by Carbuncle and her hearty brood.

By the sixth week, three pink boxes were appearing in the lounge every day, and every day the donuts were gnawed and chewed and sucked down by those whom Yxta now called the Gluttonous Fiends.

After six months of this carefully orchestrated routine, it became apparent that each of the intended victims had gained a substantial amount of unnecessary fat; however, the unintended effect was that the rest of the staff, awakened now to the sudden burgeoning of unsightly weight on their own species, commenced to swear off all kinds of sugary, creamy, fatty, unnecessary foodstuffs. Their own excess weight began to trickle off and their self-perception about themselves became clearer as their self-esteem grew stronger.

But this is not the levity of this tale.

Instead of simply refusing to eat the scrumptious donuts they had become addicted to, as if the round gobs of sugary fat were a powerful narcotic, Carbuncle and the MSs, like the monkey who puts his hand through a set of iron bars to grab a banana but then can't get the banana through the bars—and who still will not let go even as his hand swells up in size from the banging—these now-obese women would not let go of the donuts. Would these women exercise the excessive, grotesque weight off? Outrageous, these women thought. Of course, there was only one logical answer in their minds, and that was to go to a cosmetic surgeon.

Alas, these women could not deliver themselves to the butcher's knife so that he might peel away the lazy, mottled flesh off their pudgy, flabby bodies; so, instead, they had their faces done. Somehow, they reasoned, a more youthful appearance would assuage the impact of an obese body. Even Mrs. Carbuncle, who had sworn she would never have cosmetic surgery or any kind of alteration done to her face, relented.

They came back to school after Spring Break with smooth, wrinkle-free faces, just as if a heavy steam iron had been run over their fat foreheads and fat cheeks. However, there was one unintended effect of the treatment they did not anticipate.

At a meeting in her office, Mrs. Carbuncle was attempting to stuff James' career through her custom-made all-purpose butcher blender with more of her tyrannical rants.

"Mrs. Carbuncle," James said, casually, as if indeed his Principal was not threatening to destroy him as though he were a tiny bug, "are you mad at me?" If one were to close one's eyes and listen to him, one would have thought that he was guileless. "Why, your face is not reflecting the sentiment of your words. Are you just teasing me?" It now must be explained that the botulism bacterium, or rather, a weakened version of the virulent monster, had been the method of choice for Margaret and her own, and one of the residual effects for those so injected was a loss of certain facial expressions.

Mrs. Carbuncle stood, wrathful, aghast, about to explode in her frustrations toward this man, yet her face was clear, smooth, without a frown or an angry expression or any contextual clue as to her mind's intent.

"But you seem so relaxed—are you sure this isn't just a test or something?" James asked, so innocently, so nicely, and with such interest that she lost herself.

She knew he was mocking her, knew he was guiltless in his tacit innocence declared, knew she could not address his satirizing her, and those revelations drove her to a hopping-mad, lip-palpitating, drooling frenzy.

James slept happily that night.

Now, the levity, as promised, has been delivered, but the reader must be admonished that the rest of this tale will have no small amount of grim, shocking, and tragic events.

Then again, it may depend on which side of the societal fence you live.

Saffron Transforms

Celeste was sitting in her dark room, drenched in despair. James walked in and sat down next to her, holding the woman he had come to love.

He wanted to say nothing but felt compelled to say what must be said. "It's all my fault; I should never have let them see us together. Forgive me, Celeste."

Her wet, youthful black eyes, radiant and buoyant still, looked up at him and then she began to weep. She showed him the final evaluation form that would terminate her from the district.

James read it, his countenance awash in fury. "She is describing someone who does nothing all day; why, a drunk off the street who sat at his desk and read beatnik poetry to the students all year long would receive a better evaluation. I know, because I saw one of Margaret's evaluations when she was a Teacher." He smiled but it died quickly. "She has gone too far this time."

"But it wasn't Margaret who gave this to me."

A new idea was born that moment, its genesis encased in a female body that transformed instantaneously before them. A wicked, degenerate, pungent smell in the air numbed their senses.

Saffron—the woman, the familiar face, the ally, the once-supposed friend: everything now regarding her physical stature was forever altered in their minds. There was now something different about her face, but it seemed as if a dark veil that had been covering it had been lifted to reveal her true form, a form changed by her actions. Their perception of her could only have come about after a lengthy process during which she began as one person and ended as another. Her smile was still effervescent to them, but it was composed of lines and curves and angles that before had been artificially rearranged and rooted for a brief moment to serve a particular purpose.

James felt betrayal cast its steely black shadow over him. "I don't believe it," he murmured, holding still to the notion that a human being can keep their moral values while in the vile clutches of an immoral supervisor. "Why now?"

Later, he went to the room of his Mentor.

"Of course, it has been there for a while," Artemus replied that day after school as he sat in his comfortable leather chair; "you just did not want to see it."

"But you aren't even here; I mean, you are but you are not…"

Artemus smiled in a way that stated, "You know the Truth; you just have to think about it." But he did say, "I don't have to scrutinize her actions; I know how people think and the reasons they do what they do. You think about her carefully, and you will understand it. And oh," he said, innocently, "how many Teachers have you convinced about our little Secret?" Upon seeing James' embarrassed look, he laughed, uproariously. "People," he said, amusedly, "they can't help it; after all, they're just," but his smile vanished and he seemed to be thinking about the past, and then he whispered, ardently, "people."

James knew his Mentor was right about both issues, but he did not want him to be right. He consoled Celeste and thought of what some Teachers had said about Saffron this year, that she had been unreasonable to them, vindictive and unkind; but James had cast off such remarks and related Saffron's behavior to the inherent stresses of her job.

The Teachers at Amethyst Elementary—except the MSs—wanted to believe that Saffron was their shield from Margaret, that she would be their private champion, their safe haven. Without Saffron for them, all seemed lost. With Saffron against them, all was lost.

The Color of Power

A ripe, juicy red and orange fuzzy peach sits attached to its Mother Tree, admiring its own beauty but not understanding where its life-force comes from; once it falls from the green vine, it retains its lush texture only briefly, but the illusion that it can be comely forever has already been created, and it never sees its first wound of decay or its brown spots or yeast spores land upon its vulnerable, thin skin. It does not see or feel the tiny, groping insects attack its meaty pulp and suck its sugary blood. The peach still sees itself as young and vibrant and exquisite because it cannot comprehend that when one falls too far from one's intended place in life, there are no longer familiar surroundings to tell one what one should look like. To the peach, spoilage on the ground was normal, and so it reveled in it, and soon moved in with a very bad crowd, who too were rotting quickly in the sweltering sun. All of them admired their beauty and station in life, not one of them remembering their youth up in the sweet caress of Mother Tree.

As it is with the peach, so it is with those unfortunate individuals who do not see themselves for who and what they are. To surround oneself with entities who are of the same persuasion, there is no center or edge of anything, and then all things become relative.

Saffron Willow was sitting at her desk one morning during the first week of May, and she was thinking of the conflicts in her life at Amethyst Elementary School. Margaret had ordered her to issue Celeste a poor evaluation, thus depriving Celeste of further employment from the district, and many of the Teachers on campus had grown cold toward Saffron because of this. "But I cannot explain it to them that I had to do it; shouldn't they know I wouldn't do such a thing? I feel betrayed. And it was for the greater good, after all; why, look at how much good I can do for the school if I stay as Assistant Principal." But she thought of the Teachers again. "How dare they judge me? How do they know that Celeste isn't really a bad Teacher? Haven't I been trained to evaluate Teachers? Don't I go into classrooms all year? Don't I have an expertise in such matters? And maybe Celeste has problems, too; they don't know. They had just better treat me right."

But then these feelings of superiority would relent, and she would repent and nearly weep. "Mrs. Carbuncle is so cruel sometimes, but I have to work with her if I want a good review so I can get my own school; and O, then I will be fair and everyone will see that I just had to play the Game for a little while."

A student with the disposition of a spoiled, violent brat was referred to her and she had to handle his small infraction; but then an irate parent called, and Maria routed the call not to Mrs. Carbuncle, who refused such encounters, but to Saffron, who then had to listen to the cursing madwoman on the phone.

A few minutes later, Mrs. Carbuncle walked in and gave Saffron six hours' worth of work to be completed in four.

A male student, who had struck a female in the face and bloodied her nose, walked in with a triplicate referral form.

Saffron's husband called and asked her when she was coming home because he expected important company and there was much housework to be done.

Saffron could not smile and wipe away fast enough the stress that was built by several forces coming from different directions at different times with different agendas; nor could she diffuse the mounting storm of emotional strife swirling within her bosom.

This busy scene was repeated often, and was often worse, and as her husband did not aid her much in the completion of household chores, she had to let go of one part of herself to save the rest of her disintegrating sanity.

A Teacher walked in at the very moment Saffron was near emotional collapse from her inability to pour out even a vapor of her frustrations, and the Teacher asked her for a favor.

The smile was evanescent now. "And where are the reading scores I asked you for?" Saffron demanded, without forgiveness in her shrill voice.

"But I have been so busy with all the other things the district wants turned in, and my husband..." And the female Teacher halted, expecting sympathy from her own kind.

"Well, we all have our problems, don't we? It's a tough world. Get those scores in today or I'll write you up." Her pretty face was now a relief map upon which were drawn uninhabited isles and continents that no Teacher could recognize to get her bearing. The female Teacher assented, but still did not turn in the documents, and Saffron put a written reprimand in the woman's personnel file.

"These people will listen to me," Saffron fumed later that day; "those lazy Teachers, they think they can just run over me and make me look bad because I am nice; well, nice is for weaklings."

Later that day, Mrs. Carbuncle sat hunched over her desk with Yxta in front of her. "Here is your final evaluation," she said, smiling, not even attempting to mask her loathing for her.

"Unsatisfactory," Yxta said, looking at her union representative. "You need to explain yourself," she continued, icily, as if she were talking to the warden of her prison.

Mrs. Carbuncle screwed up her darting, shifting eyes and turned her small, round head toward Saffron, and said, casually, "Mrs. Willow, would you explain, please," and as she looked again to Yxta, she became excited, breathless, jubilant at the destruction of the friendship that was about to occur between the two friends.

"To think," Mrs. Carbuncle thought, not once listening to Saffron, but scrutinizing the deep sorrow in Yxta's comely face, "I can destroy a friendship as easily as if it were a clay pot dropped; O, Yxta," she was almost breathless now with anticipation, "you little fool! Saffron is mine now! I turned her against you with such ease! She was never your friend." She watched as Yxta's hopeful expression dropped. "See how quickly she has turned on you? She was never one of your kind, that is why, you stupid goose! Don't you see," she begged, as if for a moment she was actually trying to communicate with Yxta's mind, "in order for a person to become an administrator, they have to be born a leader. O, foolish girl," she raged, as if, when Yxta's countenance again fell, Margaret was even more disappointed in her, "Saffron was destined to be with my kind; she only had to be found out; but Nature is good at that." She saw Yxta's face become painful and etched in betrayal.

"You could have been one of us, Yxta, but you were weak and sentimental, and that ruined you." She felt her heart harden again against Yxta and her kind. "We never accept weaklings who would try and make everybody happy—bah! You were born to be ruled, and you're happier that way. Good!" Her eyes widened as Yxta's face flashed crimson with shame. "You understand now," she was nearly out of her seat with a wild, manic fury. "Saffron is mine! You've lost her forever! There is no turning back. She has come to us to stay!"

Saffron finished explaining to Yxta as to why she, once her friend, was now officially incompetent, and, implicit in this, that Yxta deserved to be terminated, humiliated and thrown out of the profession in disgrace.

"You'll get no letters of recommendation from us," Mrs. Carbuncle said to Yxta, squeezing more pain into Yxta's emotional wounds. "Maybe you should try being a house-wife," and she turned away, about to laugh.

"I would like to speak to Mrs. Carbuncle alone," Yxta said, strongly.

After Mrs. Carbuncle had assented, and Saffron and the union representative had left, Yxta stared at her Principal for the longest time.

"Well, what is it, what? I haven't got all day. I'm a busy woman," Margaret whined, uncomfortable now and looking about her desk for documents to read.

Yxta pulled her chair forward and placed her face directly in front of her nemesis. Her voice was strong and shimmering with righteousness. "Have you ever wondered for one moment what this school would be like if you weren't so cruel and heartless?"

Mrs. Carbuncle sat up, leaned forward and stared, with her small, gray eyes flashing outrage at Yxta. "You had better watch yourself, missy," she said, waving her arthritic, bony, wrinkled finger at her. "I haven't been really cruel to you yet."

Yxta smiled a wide, carefree smile that said, quite simply, "I don't fear you." Her face seemed fuller now, older and wiser. "But that," Yxta said, smirking now, "is the wonderful thing about meetings like this; you or I cannot prove anything about what the other said." She let her bold smile linger as if to test Margaret, and Margaret relented by sitting back and just glaring. "Good," Yxta resumed, wearing a smile of satisfaction. She pulled her black hair back as if to remove any obstacles from her words going down their precarious path to Margaret's drooping ears. "Let's talk, Margaret." She leaned back in the brown leather chair and folded her hands and laid them in her lap on top of her white Spring dress. "It is possible to be nice to people without being weak and sentimental, and treat them with respect and honor, too—and don't you know that if you did this, they would do anything for you; that is human nature: treat people with kindness and they will be loyal to you and work harder for you and defend you and care for you; why, there are people on this staff who would do anything for you if you just treated them right, but you push them away by being vindictive and petty and mean—plain old, vicious mean, just to watch people fear you." She shook her head. "I know this is a waste of time but I had to tell you because of something you long ago threw out of your body—a conscience. You are who you are, and I am who I am, and you think nothing will ever change that; O, but you are so wrong, Margaret," and she leaned closer, her face aflame with passion. "Listen, old woman, God changes things when Nature and Man both fail, you will see; and that is why I am telling you all of this—my Christian conscience compels me to, unlike any other conscience; one day you will know I was right and I will be standing before God and be blameless about my dealings with you." She nodded her head. "I am done. And oh," she said, whispering, her head slightly tilted, "I don't expect you to have understood a single word I just said."

"Oh, what a pretty speech—bah!" Margaret snarled, ecstatic that she had allowed Yxta to stay even when she knew the content of the visit, but she had only done this so she too could now be unfettered in her comments, and her voice was hard and mean and nasty, like the snarling growl of a dog bred to kill. "You're pathetic, and the shame of it all is that you could have been one of us—but instead you're one of them, a whimpering, sniveling wretch who urinates on herself every time I walk through your door. Me! All of you afraid of an old woman! Egad, what would we do if there was a war? We have produced a nest of soft lambs during this time of Peace. Maybe that is it." Her stare drifted toward the white-paneled ceiling, and her expression grew thoughtful. "During war, the weak are killed and the strong survive; what we need is a pruning, a great, cataclysmic event to begin a new era of achieving better stock in people, to beget a finer breed. Yes, that must be the answer," she whispered, rubbing her pointed chin, "yes, Malthus was right: population outruns production, and there you have it, all those idiots having idiot babies and—but what to do, what to do about it all—perhaps a famine, a great famine, yes, a great depression, to shear the weak and poor, who hang on us and steal our wages and drag us down…" but when she looked up from her reverie, Yxta was gone.

"Humph!" she grumbled, and promptly forgot what she had been doing and continued on with the final evaluations for her Teachers.

Dare to Dream

The third year of the reign of terror at Amethyst Elementary School began during a sizzling, humid, smoggy day, when all of the Teachers there felt helpless within as well as without.

"Why can't everyone simply leave," Maria said, as she sat at her desk behind the gray marble counter, downcast, as she looked at the office of her tormentor; "it isn't right, the way she blocks transfers for certain people. I want out so badly." Her face, quiet and fragile, seemed to darken. "Oh, my goodness, we're like POWs."

James no longer smiled at such frivolity. He walked over to Margaret's office and pointed to the top of the brown wooden doorframe. "Commandant," he said accusingly, and as he turned round, Maria saw a stream of red anger screaming about his hard face. "Something needs to be done," he said, walking back to her. "She has destroyed this school by chasing out veteran Teachers and replacing them with subservient, frightened young ones, and keeping the rest of us here to destroy our careers."

"Have you been able to convince any Teachers about the Secret?"

"No," James said, ashamed, "they haven't been pushed far enough."

Maria smiled knowingly. "But you and I and Yxta know, don't we? But still, I should not have to use it, it isn't right— and I know I should use it, I know, but…" She wanted to weep.

James looked left, then right and, leaning in closer toward Maria, he whispered, his voice full of mischief, "You know what she needs," and he nodded toward the office of the

Principal, "she needs one of those electronic bracelets around her ankle so we can track her." He saw Maria smile and this was his cue to turn up the amperage on his lampoon. "Really, she needs it on her so we know where she is all day," and he mimed, holding up an imaginary device in his hands as he stared at it, "yes, yes, here she comes, she is coming our way; everyone, battle stations! Or, at least," he watched as Maria began to assume a posture of mirth again, and he smiled, "at least put a bell around her neck, for goodness' sake; oh," and he issued a stealthy gaze about himself again, "but like the wise old mouse who said, 'that is all very good and well to devise such a plan, but who will put the bell on the cat?'" And the both of them laughed so long and hard it was as if their joy would set up a miraculous wall of Goodness that would, like a tidal wave, sweep down the corridor and flush out any bad thing coming their way. "Oh," he said, recovering now, "there was something I wanted to tell you from last year, about the time sheets; you know that normally we have an 'SB' next to our name for school business when we have meetings during the day? Well, she," and again he nodded toward the office, "on one of her days she wasn't here, there were the letters…"

But then the sticky, chewy voice of their Executive Boss careened down the waxed and buffed hallway, the same way a fearful trumpet heralds doom to all who hear its squealing, nauseous pitch. Of course, it must be understood that Margaret had never left the school for any reasonable length of time during the Summer. The longest stretch she was away from her kingdom was three days, and that was to attend a funeral. School was her idyllic hideaway, her fantasy mansion; there was no reason for her to leave her Paradise.

James stood firm next to Maria as Mrs. Carbuncle walked swiftly by them, this Principal who always felt that anyone in her presence must know that she was their Mistress and that fear was the leash that she yanked to make them obey.

She came out of her office in a rush. "Maria, we don't pay you to gossip. Get to work," she barked, glaring at James, and then she moved back into her royal suite.

James had already taken out a piece of paper and scrawled the last segment of his satire on it, and handed it to Maria. It read, "It had the letters 'TB,' which stands for Terrorist Business," but he had also added, "P.S. Remember not to spill water on her: Fate is not yet done with her—and the cleanup would be a mess!" He bit his lips as he watched Maria almost destroy the whole moment of secrecy by nearly laughing aloud, and then he silently retreated out through the library doors, smiling like the brave little mouse that had just belled the mighty cat.

The Breath of the Dragon

Margaret no longer confined her encrusted, foul rudeness to private meetings, for now she flaunted her unchecked Power much like the voracious cougar who raids unguarded, sleeping sheep.

The first faculty meeting of the year occurred in one of the rooms of the MSs, a place sterile of imagination and run like a laboratory that performs vivisection on newborn puppies.

Mrs. Carbuncle stood in front of her staff and spoke to them as does the despot who has finally solidified Power. "This is a school, and it's a business as well, like it or not," she cried, and she turned toward Saffron, who stood at the right hand of her Empress, and who nodded, accordingly. When Mrs. Carbuncle looked to her Teachers again, her face was thick with a boastful purpose. "There is entirely too much jaw-jacking." She smiled and spoke to herself, "I love that word," and then continued on, "there is entirely too much," and then she emphasized the next word, "gossiping," and gave a protracted stare to her attentive audience, "around here when there should be working; too many Teachers are loafing in the lounge before and after school when they should be preparing lesson plans for the next day." Her face was like an iron mask that glowed hotter as she spoke. "From now on, you will not waste the time of the classified personnel when you should be doing what you are getting well paid to do." She stared hard at them, waiting to pounce on any gainsayer. Now, she was exasperated, as if she could read the growing remonstrance in their minds. She flung her hands in the air. "I don't even care if they're on a break—you leave them alone; they have plenty to do." She frowned as if she were talking to children. "Do you hear me? I know you're thinking that big, bad Mrs. Carbuncle is being mean, but it's for your own good—don't you see that? Am I making myself clear?"

Her loyal cheerleaders regurgitated her words, and Mrs. Carbuncle stood, waiting for a challenge.

For two years she had done what she could to see what she could do, and now she knew what she could do, so she was doing it. She was doing it not because it was right or necessary or legal, but because she could. She was like the lioness who stalks the wildebeests, and who eventually realizes that its game does not flee or resist but falls down obediently and fearfully. Such behavior simply emboldens the lioness, who begins to kill indiscriminately.

"It's all for the children, you know that," she said, her face stern.

"All for the children," one of her loyalists echoed.

James gave a picture to Yxta that showed Margaret with a nose that was growing around the globe. Yxta laughed inside herself.

"Now, I want to make it perfectly clear," Margaret began, "that any student who comes in after October does not have his test score counted, so I want you—no—I am telling you, that's right, to ignore that boy or girl, just like you would a passed-out drunk on the street," dismissing said drunk with the chop of her hand in the air. "It's the fault of the parents to enroll students late—and, so help me, Hannah, if I catch a Teacher putting one of these students in a small group— you know ol' Mrs. Carbuncle will be walking around with a list of students who enrolled late…" She shook her head in disgust, and then continued on, "And as for those subjects not tested, I don't want Science or History—and you just forget the Visual and Fine Arts, too, by the way," and she raised her hands and wiggled her fingers and scrunched up her face in scorn, "those 'highbrow' activities don't put meat on my table—none of them should be taught but more than a few minutes a day, and keep writing to a minimum, too— except for the grade level that is tested for it; and as for Phys. Ed., why, just push that to the end of the day for a few minutes," and when some foolhardy person objected to her sawing off the minutes of required time for physical education, she barked, "O, phooey! Just do what I am telling you—it isn't our job to get these students in shape, but it is our job to get high scores for this school. You teach what is on the test and only what is on the test and I'll be happy and your students will be happy and you will keep your job—now, do you understand that, or do I have to waste my valuable time and put it in a memo?" And as she began to walk about again, her topic shifted as surely as if she had tossed a multitude of ideas into a fierce headwind and then begun to rant based on the first one that came back and slapped her in the face. "And you know Mrs. Carbuncle does not believe in suspensions; you need to take care of your own problems. If a student is acting up, you need to find out if you're meeting his or her needs."

Amethyst Elementary School, at recess, resembled a city in a war zone that was being looted more than it did a well-regulated place wherein children were supposed to be relaxing. Students knew there were no repercussions for their misdeeds, and so they acted accordingly.

"And I want all the Teachers to teach the same thing at the same time on the same day, just in case anybody walks in here and they want to know what is going on in the classrooms."

Few of the veteran Teachers could restrain their incredulous looks. One of them said, without checking himself first, "What about academic freedom? And it makes no sense to do everything at the same time because classrooms move at different speeds based on the overall intellectual level of the group."

"Academic freedom?" Mrs. Carbuncle responded, with a miserable frown, her voice rising in pitch. "You have the freedom to leave this school district if you don't like my orders; and as for your other excuse, why, you just make sure those kids are as smart as the next group. I don't care if you use osmosis, just get it done."

James, ever vigilant against the probing eyes of his supervisors, surreptitiously passed a note to Yxta, who presently read the following:

"Principal: noun. 1. The part of the tick that stays imbedded in its victim after it has been burned off with a match. 2.

Sometimes called a chigger, but most often associated with parasites and flies or any other tiny nuisance."

Mrs. Carbuncle, at one click of the clock appeared in one area of the room, and then at the next swish of the second hand forward, just seemed to appear in another region, and was standing right next to James, her wrinkled old hand stretched out to him, her countenance a deep magenta color, several anger-layers deep. "Give that to me," she demanded.

James, taking the note from Yxta, handed a folded-up paper to Mrs. Carbuncle, who swiftly opened it, promptly lost the color in her face as it blanched a boiling hot white, tore a wicked glance at James, and crumpled up the paper.

"You aren't going to read it?" James asked casually, his tone suggestive of a man who conquers often and conquers well. Upon seeing her reluctance to accede to his request, he dared to voyage to where no man should ever go. "The Teacher takes the note from the naughty student and the audience doesn't get to see or hear what the suspect did? Haven't you condemned the suspect with your silence?"

To venture inside Mrs. Carbuncle's core arteries at that precise moment, one would have been overwhelmed by the dynamic pressure and pounding and frantic surges of her sludgy, thick blood as it raced toward its ghoulish master, her revved-up, flabby heart.

In her raging mind, she pounded the last steel nail into James' wrist to hang him on a wooden cross and planted him directly in the middle of the playground.

Upon her twitching face, however, was written an admonition in the plainest language for him to "leave off."

James disregarded her hostile signature. "You've accused me of an unprofessional act, and I demand satisfaction."

"Mr. Yost, you need to go to my office right now," she screamed, her entire face twitching. "Get out of here, you idiot Man," she cried, forgetting herself, and before she could sputter more invectives against him, Saffron stepped in and calmed her.

James refused to move. "I'm going to call the Superintendent and the President of the Union down here right now to force you to read that note." His voice was strangely calm, his face strong and full of certitude.

As if to fulfill a prophetic utterance, the Superintendent and the President of the Teacher's Union, going from school to school, as they sometimes did throughout the year, walked in. Saffron spoke in a composed manner, explaining the situation, once again rescuing Mrs. Carbuncle from an emotional meltdown where she would have exposed all of her prejudices and hatreds against Teachers.

Of course, James had planned the whole affair, knowing that the Union President and the Superintendent were coming, but he had not counted on Saffron shielding Carbuncle.

The Superintendent, certain that Mrs. Carbuncle had damaging evidence against one of her Teachers, took the paper from her hand despite her protestations and gave it to the Union President to read. It was, indeed, a mistake, exposing the Superintendent for the man he was, a true incompetent who was incapable of intellectual thought.

"Mrs. Carbuncle is the best Principal this school district has ever had! She is such a strong woman!" the Union President read aloud, feeling these dagger-tipped words dig deep wounds into the embarrassed Superintendent.

The Superintendent then read the note aloud, as if in disbelief, and then brought Mrs. Carbuncle and James into his office, along with the now-smirking Union President.

James passed by Yxta and with great stealth dropped the real scandalous note into her waiting hands, and she presently disposed of it. He turned to face his fellow Teachers and proclaimed with jubilation, "One day all of us will be free!"

A written reprimand was drawn up and placed in James's personnel file, and he was threatened with a two-week suspension, pending an investigation of the events. Of course, the suspension never transpired.

A man stands hapless before the mighty dragon and feels its heavy breath bear down on him and he knows this is the signal for a fiery death. Think of the dragon as an employer, and the man as an employee, and in most cases, the employee will fall down and assume the fetal position, whining and moaning and despairing of his fate.

Curiously, James did not fear the fire to come; somehow, he knew the red-tinged flame would not burn him.

The Kindly Janitor

It must be said that Margaret C. Carbuncle did not concentrate her energies solely on the Teachers and their performances in the classroom; it was not only test scores that she fretted and fussed about, but the lives of everyone on campus. In every moment, in every direction they went, in every motion they made, in every action they took she wanted to be there to inspect it and direct it and modulate it. She wanted them at all times under her narrow microscope, squirming under the red-hot glare of her magnified Power. She needed to feel their weak bodies moving closely around her giant presence or she would panic and whine and then search them out until she found them and made sure they were doing exactly what she wanted them to do.

She simply could not stand to see anyone not put every ounce of strength and vigor into their job that she did; she demanded that they come early and stay late and sacrifice everything and everyone and forsake all things in order for the school to look and be radiant so that she, Margaret C. Carbuncle, might gain glory from it. Everyone had to live and suffer and die, if need be, for her vision, a vision she and she alone wore on her heart and mind and her long-ago-cre-mated-yet-undead soul; everyone must be like her and think like her and do like her or they would suffer the consequenc-es of her unequivocal, maddening, unstoppable wrath.

But there was at least one man who did resist, and he resisted openly, too. It was a curious thing to see, even from a distance, the interaction between the old man with the broom and the old steamroller of a woman, as they met and fought their daily battles.

He had worked as janitor for nigh thirty years, and he had seen nearly everything a man dares to see and had done nearly everything a man dares to do, and as he swept his way through his long career, he had seen nearly every kind of principal and every kind of superintendent and every kind of Teacher and parent and child. He had seen nearly all of it and he knew what was to come, and he was not afraid; he was not afraid because over the years, he had spun all the proper loops and lines and circular webs about himself so as to detect anyone coming at him from every conceivable angle for any reason, sane or insane. He had fashioned this care-fully constructed life-web the last sixty-two years through trial and tribulation as he ventured all over the world and with every friend and family and foe; whenever someone approached him, he could sense where they were in his com-plex, silken web, he could feel their subtle vibrations, he could sense their direction, he could discern their motives;

so, when Margaret would happen upon him, she was merely another visitor who stumbled unwittingly into his invisible personal radius and then became another hapless creature who could not mask her true intentions and wound up slipping and sliding down the slick slope into his teasing smile.

His walk was slow and steady and sure as he arrived in the early a.m. to start his rounds at the school; his large, slender black hands would open the gates and unlock the doors of the rooms and then he would set about his business as he had done for so long, but with a carefully calculated purpose and affability and professionalism and remarkable competence that had won accolades from past principals and Teachers and parents and students and everyone else who came within his small sphere of kindly influence.

He had done the same thing at the same time with such exact precision for so long that his actions were nearly seamless as he moved from one station to the next. The school never seemed dirty or unbroken or disorderly because he was always fixing things or mopping up messes or having chairs put up or taken down or leaves swept up or trashes emptied or crises averted because he was always anticipating, intercepting, calming the storm before it broke. It was sometimes difficult to see just what he did so magnificently and smoothly, unless one stood from a distance and followed him and analyzed his every move and nuance. But one had to know what to look for, or one might be fooled into thinking that he was simply ordinary.

It was a fiery red sky of dawn that sank down and gave way to a fine, sparkling, electric-blue-sky day when Margaret was traversing the perilous ground between buildings, but it was only perilous for her due to the small creatures who inhabited the magical land of the playground with its inviting white-boxed hopscotch and yellow-leather tether ball and sandy white beach replete with slippery silvery slides and rainbow-colored monkey bars.

She was walking quickly, her birdlike head looking about at all the commotion, her distaste for this chaos written plainly on her skulking countenance, when two small children came up to her and hugged her with all the purity and innocence of their youth. "We love you, Mrs. Carbuncle," the children said, in unison.

"Eh, what is this?" she cried, aghast that she had been so assaulted by the very human beings she had been selected to serve and protect. She looked behind and about herself and grabbed the children and tore them away from her aquamarine dress, and addressed them with scarlet rage coloring her words. "You children need to have manners; I am the Principal of this school." She looked at them as if they were ruffians who had purposely assaulted her for some kind of sordid gain or malicious purpose. She looked with contempt at their quizzical faces, her bony hands on her bony hips. "Don't you have any manners, you naughty children?"

But the children merely raised their small arms in a sorrowful pose. "We just wanted to hug you," the little boy said.

"We just wanted to hug you and tell you we loved you," the girl said, smiling.

"Well," Margaret responded, looking about now at the playground supervisors, "it isn't my job to hug you; go hug your mother."

"But we haven't any parents, we are orphans," the girl lamented.

Margaret looked at her carefully for a moment. "You're a queer one," she said, nearly in a whisper, "and you talk funny, and you look familiar," and she looked the children up and down and sideways and every other way of the compass her skewed vision demanded. "And your clothes are old fashioned and funny looking—why, they look like peasant clothes; you need to dress properly, you ridiculous ragamuffins."

The children raised their supplicating arms up to her once more, their innocent faces imploring for succor.

But she was soon bored with this conversation, and the many kinds of mischief her subordinates were into began to gnaw at her as she agonized over investing valuable time in idle talk. "Just go away," she said, with the wave of her hand, and she turned round to continue her walk, ignoring them just as if they were of little human value or consequence. She walked away wishing that her proposal to abolish recess would soon be authorized. "It is such a waste of time," she had said at the last meeting with her joyless masters. "It doesn't raise test scores; let the brats play at home." None of her superiors at the District Office had disagreed with her.

The two children looked after her with great sorrow, and then held each other's hands, and walked slowly away, and were never again seen on the playground.

Margaret walked over to the Yard Duty Supervisors and took out a stick of white chalk, drew a line around each of them and then scolded them for standing in one place for so long. She then threatened and ordered them to circulate about the place and keep their lazy eyes open and do their job properly or she would terminate them all. She demanded that they walk quicker from the lounge to the playground, and insisted on timing them right there and then to see if indeed they could increase their locomotion. She walked away energized and greatly amused to have had grown women dancing like obedient puppets on her taut master strings.

She was walking round the campus, on the prowl for infractions of the law of Carbuncle, looking for trouble and dirt and finding it here and there and anywhere, and knowing that if she did not find it, she would invent it.

She stopped right outside the cafeteria and peered inside with her now-flickering, canary-colored sclera—jaundice had set in but she was too mean to acknowledge it—and she nodded her head in satisfaction when she saw the janitor standing idle. She checked her watch and marched through the doors as if she were a general on her way to battle.

She walked right up to the tall, slender man just as if he were another child on the playground. Her voice was saturated with irritation and vexation. "Why are you standing here? You've been standing here for two minutes now, doing nothing, when you could be doing something; now, get to work!" She rarely addressed the classified personnel by their surnames or any other name, as her modus operandi of attack was to concentrate all of her venom on one person and by doing so stab them with her harpoon-like voice so that there was no doubt she was speaking to them.

Henry, unmoved, turned his head to look at her and acknowledge her presence with a shake of his round head as he stood with his large hands on top of the broom handle, and then he once more watched the children as they scrambled to select their foodstuff from the food stations. "The little darlings do enjoy their lunch, yes, indeed," he said, nodding affectionately. One of the little girls came skipping up to him, tray in hand, gave him a big embrace, and then skipped back to the food line. "Children, they are the most wonderful of God's creatures; so resilient against the abuses of the world, so innocent, so forgiving…"

"What are you babbling about?" Margaret cried, vexed beyond reason as her blanched face witnessed this remarkable scene. "I am talking to you; you need to get to work and quit worrying about what these children are or are not doing."

Henry smiled. "That little girl there, the one who just came over here," he said, never once looking at the woman who stood next to him, "she lost her father just, well, about a month ago, and she hugs me just about every day; I guess she needs that hug more than most."

"That isn't our concern, now, is it?" she said, scowling. "We aren't in the business of finding out the business of these students; we are here to do our respective jobs, and yours is to stick to your schedule and your prescribed janitorial duties. You spend too much time talking to students and standing around watching other people work."

"Well," he hummed, still not looking at her, "the world, the world is such a place," and he shook his head and took off his cap and scratched his short, black hair.

"Get to work, get to work, do you hear me? You loafer, you terrible slacker!" she shouted, frustration puncturing her equilibrium.

He stood there, nodding, unmoved, still looking at the children, waving at them as they waved to him and only to him, and none of them waving to her at all, as if she were not there or was totally unrecognizable to them; as if, to them, she was one of those animated gargoyle stone creatures they had heard about in fairy tales who gobbled whole little children. "A friend of mine," he began, looking and waving at his small and loyal fans, "was in charge of a big company, a big, big company, over five hundred employees, if I recall correctly; a rich man he was, too, having no complaints about money that I can recall." She attempted to interrupt him but he skillfully ignored her and continued on. "Well, it came time for him to retire and he thought and thought about it for the longest time," he gesticulated about, "and he talked to people and read books on it and thought about it, and even took off some time to see what it was like. Now," he said, and smiled, then, a genuinely large smile of affection remembered, "wouldn't you know it, that he got lost in what he was supposed to do; yes, indeed, he sat and sat at home and couldn't seem to find himself or what his purpose was outside of his work. And I will tell you how it all came down one day; well, one day," he grinned in remembrance, his round head gently bobbing up and down, "he was at the grocery store and he was in an aisle and he could not figure out the price of a can of peas, so he asked one of the youngsters there to find it out for him," he said, waving his finger, "but no, no, the youngster must have got waylaid along the way because he never did make it back to my friend. And so my friend goes up to the manager, expecting him to somehow know who he was and how important he was to the community, and he says to the manager that he is not happy with the service in the store, and that he wants satisfaction; and the manager, well, you know," he nearly laughed, smiling largely as he nodded his head and gestured about with his hands, "he apologizes, and says he will take care of him, just as if my friend was like any other ordinary man." He paused, but not for very long. "And wouldn't you know it, my friend went home that day and decided that outside of his work, he was just like everybody else, just some old man who needed to know the price of a can of peas in the grocery store and who wouldn't get any better service than anybody else—yes, indeed, just another man, nothing so special. So, he went back to work and stayed there and never left until they found him dead one night behind his desk. I guess," he said, pausing even longer to see if his incredulous audience would dare interrupt now, "he had become his job, the poor soul."

Margaret was nervously checking her watch when she finally declared, with great force, "Are you done with your ridiculous story? You need to get to sweeping, and right now!"

Another small creature with walnut-brown-colored, curly hair and a silly smile came running up to him and gave him a big, happy-to-see you hug, and then turned round and skipped happy-go-lucky back to the line.

"Write that child up for running," Margaret screamed to the Yard Supervisor on duty, who was near the food stand, and then she turned her mean attention again to Henry. "You're insubordinate now! You are refusing to get to work on my orders!"

Henry casually lifted up his left arm and spied his watch. "Well, I guess my break is over," he said, nodding his head, and slowly walked back toward the lunch line, receiving so many smiles and hugs and hellos that it created a rainbow of love all over the cafeteria.

However, there was one area the scarlet-drenched, pumpkin-colored seeds of joy and happiness fell upon but melted before they could reach the ground, a dark and brooding spot that burned a powerful stench with its poisonous menu of fire and brimstone, an acid-soaked zone flickering with hues of sulfur and a smutty, grizzly black; in point of fact, this gruesome spot launched its own dagger-pointed missiles in the direction of this spouting joy, but were soon cut down by bright orange curlicues and sparkling red squiggles and ribbons of electric green and dancing yellow. This horrible spot was uninhabitable and unimaginable to the children until the sulking, babbling old woman with the face of a gremlin and the heart of a miser went away, and then the entire cafeteria was purified by a symphony of silly grins and unrestrained laughter and a cascade of smiling brown bears and silver spirals and glistening pictures of mommy and daddy and anything else that was made in love and joy and pure innocence.

Maria Whips Her Tail

Every day that Mrs. Carbuncle came quickstepping down the highly polished tiled hallway toward her office, the heart of Maria began to quickstep down the highly polished diamond road that led to the sweet, sweet embrace of Heaven. Every day her entire being was disrupted, from her posture to her thoughts to her memories to her blessed inner sanctum from which all bad things had always been kept; but now Mrs. Carbuncle had invaded this inner sanctum through the art of attrition. Every day, Maria was fighting a battle for an army she could not see but knew was there, for an army who was attacked but who was attacked after her, for an army that hurt but hurt far less because she received the worst of it all. Maria walked point for the entire school, and daily she received the incendiary barrage from a woman who had been unleashed from all civility and manners.

Maria would be on the phone talking to a parent, explaining school policy in English or Spanish, soothing the hysterical mother, calming the angry father, winning them over with her tranquil, joyous character, and the barbed tentacles from within the royal seat of Power would start to slither and slime along the blue carpet toward her.

"Maria," Mrs. Carbuncle would yell, having overheard every word Maria had said by aiming her extraordinary batlike hearing at the school secretary, "get off that phone and get to work!"

"Oh, yes, Mrs. Carbuncle," Maria would reply, and apologize to the person on the phone and then hang up.

A Teacher might come by and ask Maria about a message he had received from a parent, and Maria would explain, and perhaps offer more information about school matters.

Mrs. Carbuncle, she of the rodent-radar ears, would come out of her viper's nest and assault the two conversationalists. "You two need to spend your time on work-related issues! Maria, get in here!" The scowl on her face would keep Maria in its egregious glare all the way into the office. It was at such times that Mrs. Carbuncle would simply give Maria a verbal lashing to further inflict more wounds upon her. "Where are those letters you were supposed to translate into Spanish? And why are your lunch breaks over the thirty-minute time limit?" When Maria attempted to reply, Mrs. Carbuncle, her countenance agitated, would wave her off. "I don't want your silly excuses, just get the work done, and stop stealing company time! Now, get out there and get to work!"

Maria never lost her composure under such circumstances.

One day, a small, slightly-hunched-over, elderly gentleman in the customary power suit of pinstripe, navy blue, came waltzing in through the front doors and commenced to walk past the front desk.

"Excuse me, sir," Maria began, following typical protocol, "may I help you?"

The man continued walking past her as if she were a tiny bug that had happened to acquire speech and had landed upon the front countertop.

"Sir," Maria said, cordially, "may I help you?" But the insolent little man continued walking on toward the library, and so Maria said, more forcefully, "Sir, I really need to ask you to state your business…"

The man, incensed at the first word she had directed at him, marched into the office of the Principal, merely cleared his flabby throat, and pointed toward the bewildered school secretary, his face as hot as coals in a twenty-log fire.

Mrs. Carbuncle came running out. "I am so sorry, Mr. Bisquit," she began, nearly smiling, "our secretary is a bit forgetful; she needs to study the faces of the Assistant Superintendents. It won't happen again." The small man with the long, pointy nose and chalky face nodded his head and proceeded to walk again toward the library, not once looking at Maria.

When the man with the lumbering gait had disappeared, Mrs. Carbuncle ushered Maria into her office and slammed the door. "If you ever humiliate me like that again in front of any of my bosses, I will have you fired, you stupid fool!" But so full of wrath was she that she could say no more, and so she let Maria leave.

Maria cried in the bathroom.

Day in and day out and week in and week out and month after bloody, terrible, awful month, Maria took the flak from the general, took it in and lay on it and kept its virulent mess from hitting elsewhere; she did it every second and every minute and every nervous, hang-wringing hour without a whimper or a cry or a curse in front of others. Every day she was crucified by Mrs. Carbuncle in the day, and every night she rejuvenated herself and came back into school with the cheery disposition that the situation had to get better.

Visitors would come in to see students, psychologists and social workers and relatives, and Mrs. Carbuncle would confront them and be rude to them and brush them away with her scrunched-up, sour face, and Maria would be the one to clean up the mess and help the people to their destination.

Every good thing that tried to live around the office was caught and tortured in between the hard teeth of the unflinching woman who sat in the insular membrane of unchecked authority. Parents came in with cupcakes to celebrate their child's birthday, and Mrs. Carbuncle would tell them that such affairs were not school business and they could take their complaints to the district office. Parents came in with ideas about assemblies to stimulate the joy of learning for the students, and Mrs. Carbuncle would tell them that the students must not lose instructional time. Parents came in to talk to Mrs. Carbuncle about fundraising for field trips, and Mrs. Carbuncle told them to get out. And Maria had to be the one who stroked the pain of those Mrs. Carbuncle trod upon—it was always Maria who held them and calmed them and gave them words of wisdom.

It was on a late Friday, when the week had already been too long and the day too long and the weather too cold, when Maria began to feel the tender squeeze of the thorny tentacles once again forming around her neck. She heard the rumbling and grumbling and muttering inside the musty tomb wherein her boss resided, and she heard the seismic, guttural pangs slamming and obliterating the small office. "Maria," the animal-like noises finally proclaimed, after metamorphosing into human language, "get in here this instant!"

Maria walked in, like a lamb into the den of the seething wolf.

"I asked you for that letter this morning about the school funds, now where is it? I have to have that down at the district office by five o'clock." It was a lie, of course; nearly everything she said about deadlines of funds or school-related items was a lie, principally, because she was the only person who knew whether or not she was telling the truth. "Now, you little fool; I want that letter or you can look for another job."

Maria calmly went to Mrs. Carbuncle's computer and casually pulled up the document she had sent her. She stood back and watched as Mrs. Carbuncle looked at the document.

"You idiot, you should have told me you were going to send it to me on the computer." Maria, once again, pointed to an email that stated Mrs. Carbuncle wanted the document sent as soon as possible through the computer. Mrs. Carbuncle nearly flushed with embarrassment. "Oh, go on and get out of my office, you little idiot!"

Instead, Maria did what no one had ever done: she did not leave immediately, but shut the door; she then turned round and with a highly resolved look on her strong and proud, swarthy face, her noble bearing and proud Mexican heritage on high, she said, boldly and without care, "You can't treat me like a dog all of the time and expect me to take it; you can't treat me like this every day and expect me to sit there and nod my head when you do not respect me. I am good at my job and you never acknowledge it. If you want me to quit, I will; but if you are not going to fire me, then leave me alone and let me do my job, and show me respect." Then, she opened the door and walked out.

After that, Mrs. Carbuncle continued to whittle away at Maria, but in a tone that was a slight degree less cold, a slight tone less harsh, in a harsh manner less attacking. But it was already too late, for, as we already know, Maria had already gone to James for the Secret, and she was now ready to join the exclusive club in their homegrown Paradise.

The Invasion

In order for an employee, in this case, a Teacher, to successfully play the Game, he or she must adhere to strict rules; to step for one nanosecond outside of the delicate boundaries set up in the provisions of the unofficial Rule Book on how to execute the Game meant certain disaster for the Teacher. Of course, there really is only one Golden Rule to follow, and it is to be invisible.

There is only one danger in being invisible—if the Supervisor unmasks your invisibility after you have so long basked in its seeming invincibility, you may go perfectly mad. But this unmasking is so rare that it is inappropriate to speak of its danger, yet.

As it is, invisibility is really a joyous state, for it gives one an anonymity on the job that ensures a peace of mind, albeit artificial.

To play the Game and achieve total invisibility, one must diligently observe several explicit rules and notions, chiefly the rule that states one must never, ever speak anything in the presence of a supervisor unless one is specifically asked to do so; and if one must speak, one must give answers in a general manner that offers nothing concrete or negative about any subject or anybody, so that the brain of the supervisor becomes befuddled and fatigued. The supervisor will then leave you, forgetting they ever talked to you. This is the key.

Nor should you ever be in the presence of your supervisor unless you are specifically asked to be; veteran employees regard the office of the supervisor the same as a leper ward.

Finally, one must never argue or question any order your supervisor gives you, no matter how absurd or how far afield from sanity it is; of course, it is always best to nod one's head, if required, and simply walk away, whether one is set on carrying the order out or not; and if one is not, be certain that the supervisor cannot find you out.

Every veteran employee knows that supervisors cannot possibly be everywhere checking up on everybody for every little thing every employee is supposed to be doing; thus, employees are able to blow off the great majority of trivial orders, and therefore keep a reasonable facsimile of their dignity. The greatest words of wisdom ever spoken in any employee's lounge room are this: "It is the quiet ones who survive."

And then the diabolical It came.

The legislators in California, in their infinite capacity to misunderstand most intellectual issues, but especially those issues relating to public schools, passed a law, and one greedily signed by the Republican Governor, that made it lawful to put video surveillance cameras into every public classroom in California.

The fateful day the law was passed, every principal and superintendent and school board member in the state suddenly felt a great surge of immeasurable Power flowing through their rusted, corroded, amoral arteries.

"Oh, it be like the movies," Margaret said, freely mocking an ignoramus, the first day the surveillance equipment was installed, and as she rubbed her dry, bony hands together, her tired, gray eyes acquired the sparkling glint that comes from the dying embers of capitulation from her enemies. Her face became gruesome dark with the light of the future, and her voice was choking on the scent of fear that poured forth from her slaves. "Veni, vidi, vici," she laughed, then, in the lush solace of her office as she observed the ten small televisions with their split screens, a cackling laugh elevated to the level of hilarity due to its grandiose wickedness that no Teacher would ever want to hear, for it was an augury of their imminent doom.

It was no longer possible for any Teacher to play the Game, and every day that they taught with the surveillance cameras peeping over their shoulders, they felt their nakedness and their shame increase.

There was a script now that Mrs. Carbuncle had labored on for months as she anticipated this new legislation, and as there had been little academic freedom for Teachers in the public schools before the new law, and now there was virtually none, she had every right to implement her script in every classroom and expect to see it performed to the very letter of her rigid rules. In addition to Science and History being on the list of subjects reduced to the minimum in her classrooms, she put out directives outlawing the teaching of or sharing of any story other than those to be found in the District-approved Reading Series, a series that had more pictures in it than words, a collection of stories so banal and worthless that students and Teachers slept through them.

Individual freedoms for the Teachers vanished, and the Teachers quickly became like the factory worker who stands obediently beside an assembly line, putting the thick yellow laces through the tiny plastic inlets of the plastic blue shoes.

Margaret seemed to achieve the hitherto unknown status of omnipresence, anticipating Teachers' movements everywhere and thereby achieving seeming omnipotence, for she now knew whether or not they really were following her directions, what they were doing, how they were doing it, and when they were doing it.

Soon, the poor Teachers began to act like those poor lab animals that are turned into neurotics through a series of electrifying shocks during sessions of behavior therapy.

In the beginning of the video camera surveillance era, three small, colored light bulbs were sunk into the bottom of the camcorder unit. The top bulb was vivacious red, the middle was mellow yellow, and yes, on the bottom was vibrant green; if a green light appeared, this meant that the Supervisor was pleased with the Teacher's performance; if the yellow light appeared, it was taken as an admonition for the Teacher, who was then supposed to resolve whatever issue it was that was hampering their performance; however, if a red light came on, that meant Mrs. Carbuncle was on her way to your room in less than a minute's time unless the Teacher performed a miracle and resolved the matter.

At first, little anxiety flowed through the suspicious minds of the Teachers as they adjusted to the presence of the surveillance equipment, which they soon called "Margaret's Eyes," or "MEs." But then the yellow lights began to appear, but no red lights, and the Teachers grew anxious; after a month, the red lights began to appear, and when they did, the Teachers would literally jump about and lose their composure. The students, quick to figure out the meaning of the color codes, often stared at the three lights for extended periods, simply waiting for the red light to come on so they could watch, to their intense amusement, as their Teachers leapt about in fear.

After three months of red lights coming on at various times throughout the day, sometimes without rhyme or reason, and even when all seemed to be going well in the classrooms, the Teachers began to fear the red lights to the extent that whenever the blood-colored bulb lit up, they began to panic and run about in a maddened frenzy.

Some students—there are always a devious few in each room—often did specific acts they knew would bring the red lights, and celebrated their Power over the pitiful Teacher as they would watch their oppressor panic and shake and tremble.

After five months, many Teachers, as they entered their empty classrooms before school began, would squirm about and perspire and babble incoherently; and if a red signal did appear during a lesson, why, the Teachers would simply stand, shaking, immobilized, grinding their teeth, whining and moaning like a lost child in the cold, frightening, dark woods.

"Finally," one of the most astute upper-grade students remarked one day to another student while he was observing his panicked Teacher during a red-light episode, "real entertainment."

Yet, the neurotic effect of the multicolored lights followed the Teachers everywhere, and many Teachers became loners wherever they went; their marriages crumbled, their friends turned from away them, they became social outcasts.

Every Teacher—except the MSs—at Amethyst Elementary School was affected except James and Yxta, and among the classified staff, Maria seemed immune too, even though she also had a camera directed right at her.

Each day they lost precious bits of their emotional compass, and each day they grew more despondent.

The women who had lost weight during the pink box era gained it back, and grew fatter still.

Margaret and her loyal nest of vipers swore off the facial injections and the pink boxes, and their inflated bodies deflated, just like the hulking balloon figures in a holiday parade do, back to the soggy, flabby forms they had been before. The MSs met in the lounge and laughed and giggled and talked away as if they were at a resort spa; and while the misfortunes of others increased, their fortunes increased. It all had to do with an inverse relationship between Good People losing their will to resist evil, and evil people devouring the energy and desire of the Good People.

Teachers were too tired to even think about stopping the unethical idea behind the surveillance cameras, for survival became paramount to them, and not merely for financial reasons, but for emotional and intellectual reasons as well.

And even those who absolutely let go of their pride and honor and did whatever Mrs. Carbuncle wanted them to do still could not please the Ogress, and their hearts continued their downward spiral into an icy oblivion.

James and Yxta continued to exhort the Teachers at Amethyst Elementary School about the Grand Secret, and slowly, the Teachers began to listen. In the beginning, the Teachers did not understand the Secret, nor listen as they should. Soon, though, as their minds sloped toward deep, black depression, they capitulated, and one day after school, James and Yxta and Maria stood before all of them in James' room.

The Teachers listened to passionate exhortations but did they not understand, and so they continued on in their duties at school, still heading toward an emotional meltdown.

Many more of their marriages began to crumble, more of them acquired health problems, a few divorced, and two of them nearly killed Mrs. Carbuncle but changed their minds and packed up their guns and walked home and contemplated committing suicide.

Not one Teacher quit, for something in them prodded them on toward their job every day. And what was it?

There was a sublime mist that inundated the school, a genuine reality that beckoned the Teachers on, a great hope, an eternal optimism, an idea that this injustice would pass as had all other immoral reforms and attacks against them; the Teachers still saw the school as an inviolate place above society's vengeful aim, beyond the reach of corrupt politicians and bitter, idiotic journalists; that somehow the Teachers' honorable dedication and utter, selfless devotion to educating the children of the world would repulse any foreign influence.

The Teachers held steadfast and true to the noble idea that somehow the outside world cared about schools if only for the sake of the innocent children; this, too, proved false, as every day the Teachers realized that the prevailing will of power mongers and the apathy of human lemmings determine the course of direction and drive policy in the public schools. How did they know? Why, Teachers all over the state took to the streets to protest the surveillance cameras, but they were greeted with universal hostility by the media, politicians, and citizens alike. Teachers were branded as money-hungry, lazy, liberal whiners who had hidden too long behind their unions for protection against their incompetent selves.

Teachers at Amethyst Elementary School had but one hope left, a hope that had faded long ago, but one they revived in their delirium, and it was Saffron Willow.

In the Beginning

James, in his downward spiraling hope that someone, somewhere, somehow would resurrect that which was wholesome and good about education and thereby crush and defeat the fleet of cameras that daily sailed like pirates over them, sat down to write a protest letter to a large, national newspaper. "This one is for you, Maria," he had said as he mailed the letter, but as he expected, the newspaper would not publish the work, if only because he did not have the requisite PhD or other such prestigious title after his humble name. However, here is the letter, in its entirety, for the readers to enjoy.

"When one is about to relate the history of an institution to an audience, it is always best to begin at the beginning, for to do otherwise is just plain dishonest. So, here is a cursory but authentic telling of the history of education and how it devolved to allow cameras in the classroom.

"It goes something like this:

"A long time ago, so long ago that most people who are cozy about quoting school statistics of today have no knowledge of it, schools were constructed as a means to educate people (there were also some noble words about educating the citizenry to ensure that Democracy would not fail). It all sounded good and was, in fact, a very simple notion, that people should have the chance to improve themselves through education, to write more than two big Xs—if they so desired—for their name on a sheet of paper. In America, the idea of schools for the masses did not become law until the early twentieth century, when it was supposed that young children were best left in the classroom instead of toiling in filthy factories and hot fields. At that time, no one really thought that every child who attended school would become a full-fledged genius capable of reading the Great Works of Literature and of Science and History. It was thought that children might gain certain knowledge of reading and writing and math and the such, so they might have a better chance at pursuing those lofty promises written in our nation's sacred scrolls. It was the job of the Teacher to teach and the job of the student to learn, but key was that the student had to attend on a regular basis and to behave; well, there were too many children who still worked part time or just plain neglected school, and so lawmakers decided to make sure that all students attended school, and rightly so.

"School, if you will recall, in its initial premise—and even now, in its current offering—had but one goal, and that was to give citizens the proper intellectual tools so that they might thrive in society; what it could not do was promise that it could cure disease or brain damage, or wipe out crime or hunger. Education boasted that it would do its best to outfit a citizen in order for that citizen to have the best opportunity to thrive, but never was there a promise that the person would come to school and be altered economically or socially or mentally or physically, yet that is exactly what has happened. From whence came this outrageous claim that the schools must heal the sick and cure the social ills of society? It came not from within, but from without.

"No good doctor would ever boast that every one of his patients would never be ill again, nor would any parent ever boast that their child will never provoke unrest in society; no prison would ever boast that every prisoner released is rehabilitated, nor would any good coach ever say that all of his athletes will achieve the same results despite a great diversity in their physical size and ability and genetic makeup. But schools became a place where the ills of society were supposed to be passed through the magical pixie dust and where the children would go in with diverse societal ailments and come out, renewed.

"It began with state tests to test children, and from there, certain people with larger-than-normal gaps between their synaptic nerves noticed that certain countries had higher scores than American students in every level and every subject; and then these popinjays began babbling about weak American schools and how they were failing our children; but in the beginning, as even now, there were scholars who pointed out that those countries with higher test scores were only testing their crème de le crème, and that good old honest America was testing everyone; but the politicians ignored what was reality and chose to accept these poor comparisons, and the yellow journalists did too, and so the idea that schools could, in fact, erase all of society's problems came into being. If the schools of the other countries had problems in society and yet their schools managed to overcome them, the chant began, why can't we? It was like being at a football game where the frothy lyrics are made up along the way by silly cheerleaders. But this time, the cheerleaders had venom on their tongues and loathing in their hearts, and they began to cite fragments of research, and they cited the business model, too, and how successful certain businesses were in achieving their goals. So, the schools were coerced into following this peculiar mechanical model, as if the children were merely walking and breathing computers that only had to be pro-grammed by competent and caring Teachers, and then, and only then, would children truly benefit from school. If a school had low test scores, then it meant that the Teachers did not care, and if the school had high test scores, then it meant that the Teachers truly cared. And so, those legisla-tors who could not and would not blame their failed social reforms, nor blame parents for failing to raise their children properly and adequately prepare them for school, did a horri-ble thing: they signed into being a law to seal the verdict that schools alone could reform society, and thus was born one of the most wicked pieces of legislation in the history of the world, the All Children Will Learn Act, or ACWL.

"The ACWL promised that every single child in America would become proficient in the areas of reading, writing and arithmetic by a certain calendar year, and that any school that did not achieve these lofty goals would be severely pun-ished. And how did parents respond? Can you imagine the joy of parents who had mentally ill children, or children who were brain damaged, when they heard this news? Ah, but this was ephemeral, for the lawmakers soon realized that such children as these were exceptions and allowed these children not to be counted during testing; but what of the parents who had children who were just plain slow, and who could never, even in a thousand centuries, read at grade level? It is supposed that they were overjoyed; and what of the parents who did not take care of their children by not feeding them or dressing them properly or getting them to school often enough so that the child could learn? And what of the parents who were fresh on our pristine shores with children who could not read English but heard the promise that a walk through mystical fairy dust would alter all of that and transform their child into a blossoming genius in a dash? I suppose they too were overjoyed!

"And what of the Teachers who knew that schools have no magic fairy dust and that they could not possible cure every societal illness simply by using the best methodology and even the best curriculum? They were the only ones who knew the truth, and they were the only ones crucified daily, and many were vanquished.

"And what of the CEOs of industry; what of them? When their businesses failed wholesale and their practices were found faulty and full of avarice and transparent stupidity, and their morals thoroughly and skillfully corrupt, what of them? They cared not for the damage they had inflicted by their constant rant that schools were failing our children—their future human capital to make them more fabulously wealthy—for they were too busy arranging their Picassos on the verandas of their Italian townhouses while sipping from thousand-dollar bottles of wine with their French mistresses.

"And what of the yellow journalists and vindictive legislators who demanded that the ailing schools fix themselves or suffer their wrath? Well, they decided that the only way to ensure that every child in America would benefit from the great ACWL would be to have cameras in the classrooms of those insufferable Teachers, those union-clutching, liberal-leaning, coffee-drinking and pop-in-a-video Teachers. Thus, the cameras were born, and now you know why."

And so this letter said, and so it died in the recycling bin of every major and minor newspaper he sent it to, for every major and minor newspaper considered the author, this ordinary Teacher, the same way a judge considers a defendant— as a person who has testimony that is considered extremely prejudicial and prone to shameful prevarication.

But you do not know the rest of the story.

There could never and would never be a school where every child was a genius unless it was a magnet school or a private school that allowed only the best and brightest into their bejeweled rooms and golden corridors, thereby achieving high test scores; and it was at such times as these that meddling and ignorant outsiders praised such places and then pointed the accusing, dagger-tipped finger at public schools and rebuked them for not having scores of equal merit.

But there were some schools, just ordinary, run-of-the-mill, everyone-come-as-you-may schools that had a few very extraordinary Teachers who achieved the supposedly impossible and unbelievable; to wit, their students outscored every class in their school and just about everyone else on the planet. One such school was our very own Amethyst Elementary, and here are the facts.

Two of Margaret C. Carbuncle's closest allies, Hilda Schmidt and Leticia Wiggenbottom, at the beginning of this school year received hitherto unknown scores for their fifth-grade students from last year; the scores were so high and so profoundly different from the rest of the students and the general population that the State Department and the Education

Division of the Federal Government sent their best team of non-educators to investigate the matter.

But they did not come to bury these two Teachers, but to praise them. The State Department people and the blue suits from the Education Agency of the Federal Government came in armed with video cameras and happy smiles and flashy badges and gaudy plaques and lots of effusive praise for the two Teachers, and they talked and talked and applauded these two in front of the staff and the press and the parents who came there to listen to the important visitors from the parallel universe where decisions are manufactured in candy-colored offices through the thick lens of rose-colored glasses.

And what happened after the important people from the land of the myth-makers retired into that good night? What became of those left in their disarming wake? Well, the Teachers who did not have high test scores were plunged headfirst into the meat-grinding machine by the press and the parents and the administration for failing to achieve the greatness of their esteemed co-workers.

And here is how it all ended.

It ended in the office of Mrs. Margaret C. Carbuncle the night after the big people from the distant horizons had been taken into the billowy clouds by the taxpayers' blood, sweat and tears; it ended with the Principal and her two allies, and even Saffron, sipping champagne out of crystal glasses, toasting the overwhelming success of successes; they laughed and danced and dreamed of greater things for their careers, and when the festivities were nearly over, Margaret leaned over to her friends, a big, sloppy smile plastered upon her silly, wrinkled old face, and then said, giggling, "Why, it's so simple, why doesn't everyone cheat as well as we?" And the four of them laughed so loud and so long and so hard that they nearly had a state and federal conniption.

And now you know the rest of the story.

The Way It Is

It is often said that the way things are, exist so for a reason. A botanist looks into the secret life of the green forest and finds diversity that begins at one extreme end of the spectrum and runs clear to the other end of it; the zoologist looks into the green forest and sees great diversity of life, great variation among every creature as it relates to strength and physical grace and color and shape and behavior and feeding habits; everywhere the two scientists see genuinely unique species that are singularly different. What would these scientists do if, to their utter amazement, every organism within its species began to replicate itself to become like one universal species; to wit, that every flower transformed to look like one gray, plump, tall flower, and that every member of the bird family transformed to become one dull, gray, fat bird? But what if every species within a species then became robust and healthy and strong and without physical ailment, what then? What then, the scientists know, would never occur, because there is an infinite variety of life on Earth, not only in fauna and foliage but in people, as well.

People are also a species that falls within the pattern of the infinite variety of life, as it relates to strength and physical grace and color and shape and behavior and feeding habits, but in the case of human beings, there also must be considered intelligence and morals; the neuroscientist examines the human brain and sees it in terms of intelligence from one extreme end of the spectrum to the other. Every family member knows that every other member of their family is unique in their ability to reason and understand and listen and learn; every friend, regardless of their level of intelligence, understands the great diversity of intelligence among their friends. It seems that everyone on this good green planet understands that there are simply those who will never attain the same quality of intelligence as another, that there are an infinite variety of intellects and personalities and wants in people; everybody seems cognizant of these inescapable and easily discernible truths: everybody, it would seem, except for those who make the rules as it relates to public schools.

A schoolroom, then, might be seen as a microcosm of the world, a kind of indoor green forest wherein exists a great variety of life as it relates to intelligence and behavior and morals; but here, in this artificially set-up enclosure that is packed with too many students and too few Teachers, unlike the forest where it is acceptable to have a different coat for the leopard as opposed to the coat of the goat, every creature's intellectual and behavioral outcome is supposed to be the same.

It must be remembered that it was the business model that was the prevailing philosophy behind the way students were to achieve in schools, that students were likened to car parts, that they needed only to be assembled with great solicitude and expertise and they would come out sleek and fast and shiny and new; that students were like obedient little lambs who would sit innocently and proudly and await instruction if only the Teacher would teach with efficiency and precision; this, the press said, this, the politicians said, and this, the public came to believe; but this, no one in public education would ever believe—not the Teachers nor the students nor the aides nor the secretaries nor anyone else there—because they were on the campus, and they were the only ones who would ever be there.

At Amethyst Elementary School, as in every school, there existed certain classrooms that had an inordinate amount of children who were unusual. At any grade level where there was an ally of any Principal, the Teacher received those students who were unusual in that they were well behaved and highly intelligent; as for the rest of the Teachers at that grade, they received a reasonable mix of students from various socioeconomic backgrounds; but there were always, and always would be, those certain Teachers who would have an inordinate amount of highly unusual students, if only because the ensuing chaos amused the Principal. As for Margaret C. Carbuncle, she was highly amused, then, by the classroom of Thomas G. McKinley, a young man who had become a Teacher to inspire and save every troubled student within his youthful reach.

It all happened because Margaret had three allies on the sixth-grade team, and Mr. McKinley was the fourth sixth-grade Teacher; other Teachers attempted to warn him of the consequences of this unfortunate circumstance, but he simply puffed out his chest and declared that he was ready and raring to go and would do whatever was necessary to help his children. Thus, his trial began.

It began where it always begins, in the line at the beginning of the day; the sixth-grade students of the other rooms displayed an even temper and new clothes and happy, clean faces and minds as they stood in line at the strictest attention; but one had only to look a little to the left to witness the distorted, broken, haphazard mess of a sloppy line that was Mr. McKinley's thirty-two students. Fifteen of them were chasing each other and hitting each other and throwing backpacks at each other and cursing at each other, all while eating and laughing and discarding garbage onto the black-top. Mr. McKinley, blonde haired and six feet one and square of jaw and brimming with health, appeared before them in his beige denim khaki pants and white cotton polo shirt and brown leather dress shoes and an abundance of enthusiasm and optimism for their future. He advanced a stern look at them, and those good students who were caught up in this maelstrom stood at attention, but the Fifteen evinced a severe lack of obedience, and so kept up their ill-mannered behavior. Mr. McKinley lectured them about their actions and spent a few minutes shaping up their lines and then followed them to the classroom. He asked them in and watched them sit down and then he began the lesson, but then the Fifteen began their fun.

They had not come to school to learn, these Fifteen; they had never been to school to learn, as evidenced by their report cards from kindergarten to fifth grade, and now their brash attitudes were more severe, and their ability to deplete all learning within their immediate borders more exceptional. Oh, how they laughed and mocked and swore and challenged the Teacher at every point of the compass; oh, how they threw crayons and pencils and wadded up paper and hit other students and flew paper airplanes and leaned back in their chairs; oh, how they reveled in the chaos they bred; oh, how they marveled at their juvenile ability to circumvent the rules and customs of an entire civilization. They were an instant gang of collaborators to bring down the established routines and rules of their surroundings—this is the way of every mischievous youth, to combine into one whenever they cross each other's calamitous path.

But Mr. McKinley would not be broken nor bowed, and he met them head on and fought them here and on the playground there and in the office and he even went to their homes to visit their parents; yes, he was the sterling Teacher the media suggested as panacea for the troubled youths of today; yes, he was the model Teacher who was quick to abandon his own ambitions and problems and needs and instead help the troubled youth of today; yes, he was ready and willing to do whatever was necessary to guide these troubled children back to the Blessed Light.

The first stop along his route to successfully helping his students was the office of his Principal, Margaret C. Carbuncle, who promptly told him, when he wanted to punish a particularly violent offender in his classroom for various violent actions, that he, the Teacher, was the sole reason why these students were acting as they did; that he, the Teacher, was responsible for their bad behavior because of his poor classroom management; and that he, the Teacher, succeeded or failed based on his own strategies and practices. And then she once more promoted her motto, "There is no such thing as a bad student, only a bad Teacher," and sent him on his way back to an ever-widening oblivion.

So, he was now without support from the office, but, of course, these students had already learned that, and the Fifteen openly taunted the lack of authority on campus and basked in their own interpretation of immunity from prosecution; so, he took to sending the worst of the Fifteen to other classrooms on time-outs, but once Margaret C. Carbuncle found this out, she put a stop to it.

So, now he was alone with the Fifteen and it was early in the year and they were eating away at his authority and teaching just as surely as if he were a new building of wood infested with an army of avaricious termites; and so he did what he had heard from other Teachers and what he had read in education journals and books and what he had seen in the inspirational movies about Teachers and their problem students—he visited the homes of the Fifteen. Here, he reasoned, he would find answers and collapse the insurgency movement within his classroom.

And he did visit the homes of the Fifteen, and he sat on beer-stained sofas and listened to insensible rants from insensible alcoholics and he listened to frustrated parents who had no idea what to do with their delinquent children, and he listened to foster parents who feigned interest and parents who indulged their brats at every turn and who never once thought of disciplining their child for fear of making the child sad; he would find out that many of the students were foster students, and he soon realized that many of the students had been labeled as extremely difficult by the County, and that the County gave extra money to families that took in these troubled youths; he found out that many of these foster families he visited had children coming and going and others staying but leaving too soon, only to be replaced by another, then another, yet another bucket of walking and mumbling cash and then another barrel of mixed-up, messed-up, directionless money—so that no one child stayed too long, no child stayed too long and grew too old and caused too much havoc—and any little monster child that did pull the metal hammer down too many times in these houses of pain would be jettisoned back into the foster-care system. So, he found out that he had the authentic drug babies and the physically battered and emotionally battered and the ultra-violent and the plain, old-fashioned spoiled ones, and he was not deterred—no, not him, for he was young and full of hope for the future of his students, and so he plowed forward and thought about all of it and worked on it at his home and thought about it on the way to work and at work and after work and all day, every day, in every way and with everyone, he sought help and wisdom on the issue of bringing the Fifteen to salvation.

By December of that school year he had spent thousands of dollars of his own money on books and computers and electronic learning games and subscriptions to children's science and geography and history and current-events magazines and newspapers; he was at school early and left late every day and dedicated himself to inventing the most creative lessons, and he thought about his dilemma from every angle and from the children's angle and he still woke up every day determined to bring the Fifteen into the fold and nurture them back to the Light.

He bought a grand fir tree for the holidays and placed gifts there for the students and he planned a wonderful cultural feast for them and he stood proudly as he observed his handiwork and thought of all he had done for them; it was on the morning of the big feast when he admired all of it and then he went for a break during recess.

But he made a mistake when he left the room—he left the back door unlocked.

When he came back to the room, the first thing he thought of was how quickly and efficiently the Fifteen had worked to destroy the glad tidings of the room, for they had wiped it all clean; they had knocked over the noble fir and stepped upon it and smashed it and ripped it apart and thrown the sumptuous home-cooked food all about the room and dumped over the tables the food had sat upon and smashed the two computers and electronic learning games; they had smashed the video cameras in the room to avoid detection and they had even ripped and torn and smashed the gifts he had bought for each of the students; they even destroyed the gifts, he sighed, surveying the mayhem, they even destroyed that which anyone else would have stolen, he bemoaned, and he felt his heart grow heavy with doubt and woe, as if he were up against something unseen that could not be conquered from within.

When all the students came to the room, the ordinary students displayed ordinary shock and sorrow, while the Fifteen laughed uproariously at their mischief, then sat down with arms folded and arrogant smirks plastered across their too-early punk faces.

Of course, he was human, and he wanted to capitulate right there and then, and nearly did, he nearly gave in to the Fifteen, but he swiftly recovered because he was, after all, young and ambitious to help all children learn and grow toward the Light, and he was quick to forgive and forget and move forward those who were still willing to listen and learn; he called a catering service and a nursery and they brought good food and a tall noble fir and the feast went on as planned. There, he had beaten the Fifteen, he thought, watching the students serving each other their food, and he hoped they would listen and learn and regret and repent of their mistakes, and then the worst of the Fifteen began to throw their food about and another threw their food about and still another, until there was a fierce food fight and the feast was on the blue carpet. He was beaten, easily.

When Margaret C. Carbuncle found out about it all, she blamed Mrs. Willow for being too lenient with him, and him for the disaster, him for the break-in, him for the mess, him for the ridiculous attempts to create a ridiculous environment where it should not have existed; so she banned any more of his feasts and electronic games and computers, books and magazines and said that he had tempted the students to mischief; she admonished him to teach the standards and only the standards and not allow the students to watch any ridiculous motivational videos or any other such nonsense and that it would only confuse them and not prepare them for the almighty state tests; and she pummeled him about parent complaints and low district test scores and she scowled at him that the other classes were outperforming his class and that she would find someone else to do the job if he could not. She fumed about this mess for a good while, knowing it would be difficult to cheat efficiently on the state test with so many low test scores from just one class; she knew how to subtly raise test scores with low-scoring students— in fact, she had boasted about it at her meetings with the Superintendent by simply turning a pencil around and showing off the clean, pink end of a new yellow pencil; but she knew that too many erasure marks would be a red flag to the State Department of Education, so she resolved to drop the lowest students in the school from the official attendance and re-enroll them, thus giving them a date entering the school after October, and thus invalidating their state test results. She hugged herself when she thought such thoughts, as she knew there was always a way out of such ridiculous messes.

And now it was February, only halfway into the school year, and he had shot his mightiest cannon and was now out of ammunition, and he did not know what else to do; he was being harassed by the red lights and the administration for every little thing, and his enthusiasm for the Great Experiment to reach the Fifteen was dissolving fiber by fiber, and he felt as helpless as a mute old lamb that tries to sound a bleat of warning about the black wolves that are coming to devour the stupid and lazy flock.

He was a statue of salt dissolving grain by grain as the wind of chaos swirled around him—chaos like sharks swimming madly around a helpless and wounded baby seal. He could not find his bearing in this swirling tempest could not feel his moral compass in this inverted ecosystem, could not decipher the garbled code of instructions that guided a Teacher through the deadly labyrinth of what to do and when to do it and why it should be done and who should be saved and who should be excised and thrown out like a malignant tumor.

There came a long, cold and hard five days, and he was drained of his energies, he was drained of his enthusiasm, he was drained of his will to win, but still—still—every morning, the poor fool woke up and popped out of bed and threw on his clothes and ate a hearty breakfast and proclaimed that today was the day he would win them all over. And then on this Friday, at the end of a dreary week that possessed all the required ingredients to push a Teacher over the edge and bury him alive, he received a phone call in the early morning before he departed for work. His countenance dropped.

After school that day, he knocked on the door of the Principal and entered her office.

"Yes, yes, what is it, now?"

He did not hesitate at all. "I received a phone call that my father has just died."

She screwed up her eyes, and he could see in her face that she was visibly irritated, that she had intended to squawk and hem and haw, but then she said, "Well," and she paused, and said again, her voice rattling around in a cage of vexation, "well, what of it?"

"I want to take off five days." He handed her the paper that he had signed and needed to be signed by her so he might take his five days for bereavement as guaranteed in the contract.

Her mouth unhinged itself and seemed to engulf the entire room in her shock. "What? What is this? Five days off, for what?" She looked up at him as if he were the town imbecile. "Don't you know the state tests are nearly here?

Five days, five days," she recited, looking again at the paper-work, "that is too darn many to take right now. I'll have to check and see if you need that many," and then she began to stand, "and maybe you need prior approval for this, too."

"No, no, you don't." He stated it emphatically—his father had just died. "I get my five days off if I have to travel a cer-tain distance, and I don't need prior approval for the death of an immediate family member."

She looked up at him and now she stood fully erect; of course she knew the contract, of course she did, it was her business to know it, but she had wanted to scare him and worry him and throw him off balance. She looked at him now with scorn and disgust, the same way a queen looks at a slave who has just asked her to bury his wife who has been crushed by a stone block as it was being raised up the plat-form of the great pyramid wherein the queen would one day be buried. "Oh, go ahead, go, go," she growled, and then shooed him away with her right hand, which was covered with dangling bracelets, and then she abruptly stopped, and cocked her head, and said, the blood of arrogance rushing to her wrinkly face, "At least, at least," her voice was softer now, like a steel trap that has been covered in vibrant colored leaves, "I want proof of the mileage used."

"Fine," he said, and began to leave.

"And one more thing, yes," she said, rubbing her chin, "I want proof, too." She looked at him and saw his bewil-derment, and she was pleased, and she smiled inside her-self, where only those gross obscenities that lived in the dank and cold shadows resided, and then she barely spoke above a hushed whisper, "I want proof that he is really dead," and after she said it, she moved around the desk and stood right next to him, inspecting his incredulous gaze. "That's right, I want a copy of the death certificate, to know that not only he is dead, but that he died recently." She smiled, then, and folded her arms. "No one," she whispered, "pulls the wool over Margaret C. Carbuncle's eyes."

He was looking at her now not as a Teacher who looks at a principal, nor as an employee whose face wears the spittle of a profane speech by his supervisor, but as a man who looks upon a woman whom he has just decided is little more than a serpent and a lot less than a human being; he could not hide his moral outrage, he did not want to hide it, he had not learned how to, and as he walked out through the door, his grief caught up to him. He turned and nearly shouted toward the office of the Principal, and everyone in the front office heard him. "No, you will not get proof," and he walked back into her lair, "you will not get proof because I won't give it." He was staring at her and his body was trembling, and then he shook his head. "I don't need to give you proof of anything—you just made that up, didn't you?"

She laughed—she laughed like an old master who has been caught by her fresh young pupil—and then she waved him away as she walked toward the door. "Oh, just go, go to your little funeral, you big sissy; and for five days, maybe we will get someone in your room who can get some real teaching done." She flung him the document and slammed the door shut.

He was gone for those five days, and the very day he came back, she was in his room, writing him up for every little thing he was doing wrong and lying about him for every big thing he was doing right.

The Miracle

A person who betrays you can be forgiven and forgotten ad infinitum, but it is more difficult if that person is your friend. When that person betrays you to the point that you no longer see that person as someone you once knew, it is hard to forgive, and harder still to forget.

Saffron was viewing the multiplex screen in her enlarged office, glancing over the twelve Teachers she had been assigned to observe with the closest scrutiny. One moment she was typing documents, another moment she was disciplining a boy who had punched a girl in the face and had chipped her tooth, an abhorrent act Saffron could not properly discipline the boy for because her Mistress forbade suspensions unless the parent of the victim complained about the lack of punishment.

In her fomenting anger, she glanced at the screens, hoping to see someone to punish. If she could not punish naughty children or her husband for his neglect toward her, or Margaret for her emotional staidness toward her, or herself for her horrible indecisions, she would punish those Teachers who would not follow the rules as she had to. She observed two of the Teachers engaged in activities previously ascribed to good teaching standards, but now, under the law of all things leading to high test scores, such activities were deemed treacherous; consequently, she touched the two red buttons on each panel, and was amused to watch the Teachers fidget and begin to squirm. There was a moment of regret in her mind, but then she thought of her own situation. "I have to take orders and do things I don't like," she reasoned, and so she built up a wall between protecting herself and protecting Teachers. "After all, if Mrs. Carbuncle sees this and knows I did not 'red light' them, it's my job. Oh, those insufferable Teachers! How they do cause me so much woe!"

She did not remember walking in and verbally reprimanding the two Teachers she had given the red light to, but when the deed was done and she was back in her office and had looked at the clear screen and her face bent closer to observe the violators now yielding to her specific instructions, there was a sense of raw, undiluted Power welling up in her. This had always been a precursor to true Power, a waxy pump ready and willing to be changed into the potent form, but it had always died in her before it could make the change because she would not allow the conversion. She looked to the male student still sitting silently in his seat and she let loose a small injection of pure Power at his vulnerable psyche, and in a moment she had him sniveling like a whipped dog on a short chain.

After the boy departed, Saffron sat back and reflected upon this new serum of authority that had begun to fill up in her tissues and spill into her bloodstream and flood the cells of her brain. She had let it in, and had tasted its vital juices, heard its melodic music, felt its raging pulse, and she felt strength increase in her. "But why is this so bad?" she asked, not yet fully aware of her transformation. "Are things that give you confidence so bad? Oh, those philosophers who speak ill of authority, those old hermits! They condemn what they do not know or understand. I haven't felt this good about myself in such a long time—and no more crying for you, Saffron!"

Thus, she now resided in the Crystal House of Power; and in her infancy in this new home, when she did manage to look back at what she had once been, she sometimes felt there was another way for her to be; but then she would shrug her shoulders and think of the present. "How happy I am now to know I am finally who I have always been," she said one day to Margaret, whose sour face puckered up in perverted glee.

When Spring sent a hot, sweltering bubble that burst like a hot, steaming, gooey egg all over the Teachers at Amethyst Elementary School and immersed them in sweat and misery, it had already been a month since Saffron's consummate seduction by that comely groom, Power, who grew in her moist heart like a creeping green moss.

The Teachers sat in Yxta's room after school on a day when Mrs. Carbuncle and Mrs. Willow, with a wild gleam in their eyes, had issued twelve written reprimands to various Teachers.

As the Teachers bewailed their fate, James dwelt on the wisdom of Artemus, who had recently retired. "Remember," Artemus had so often said to him, "only when people ask you for advice," and he had been sure to emphasize his last words, "do you actually give advice. But don't be upset if even then," he had said, strongly, "they still won't listen."

James stood, anxious, waiting, listening to their deep anguish.

"How much longer will the cameras be down," Yxta whispered to Maria, who had sabotaged the system.

"One hour," she said.

"Tell me again," one of the older women moaned, exhausted of all her energies, "I no longer care about this job. It is over for me."

James stood, waiting for all of them to implore him.

"Please," many of them said in unison.

"It's all of us or none of us," James said, quietly.

Everyone agreed that the time was now.

"Then," James replied, his face glowing with authentic Knowledge, "listen, and you shall yet be saved." He stood fully erect, and his countenance grew grave, his brown eyes brimming with the gift of absolute certitude, his voice suffused with intelligence, and he began, slowly, solicitous to choose the right word and intonation and tone. He could feel his rich words digging into their fertile hearts.

"The time has come, my friends, to save ourselves from an unstoppable enemy so we can live to fight another day." He halted for a moment, desirous to let his weighty preface prepare the way into their muddled brains. "And where did all of this originate? How did it get so far, unchecked? I say to you," his voice thundered now, "it is unnatural for human beings to take orders or to give orders, but in our society we must do this for the survival of Democracy. We gain on one hand," he slowly lifted his right hand up; his left slowly lowered down, "and lose on the other." He paused and his face grew mighty with wrath. "Do you know why Margaret is here every day, all day until late at night? Because she can't give orders to anyone else and have them fear her! But here she is a goddess on Earth, worshipped and obeyed without question. Her kind must have subordinates, must give orders, or they die a miserable death; her kind live on the vapors of fear that pour from our steaming minds."

He shook his head. "But now we lose too much because of Margaret and her kind, and what we gain we no longer know how to measure. And we lose our pride and honor and self-respect if we care. So," his voice became an impassioned whisper, "we must no longer care." His lips pursed as his black eyebrows knit and his eyes burned bright with the revelation of golden Truth. "Did you hear me? To care is to die, now, but we must not die; no, we, on the contrary, we must live! To live is good for us and our families and our future students who one day will need us; my good friends, if we care now, they win," and he gestured toward the administration's office; "we can't do any good right now; right now, everyone loses. So," and he put his fisted hands on two desks in front of him as he leaned closer to his mesmerized colleagues, "we must live because we can't win! Don't you see! They have won for now! Our American individualism won't allow us to capitulate to anyone, but now we must admit defeat whole-heartedly, completely, without regret." He stood erect again, and his voice was drenched in urgency. "And no turning back! Once we go in, there is no going back; no sentimental weakness because the poor children might suffer! Well, they are suffering and our deaths won't help them." Their nodding heads and disheartened faces compelled him onward. "Don't you see that they have won? Carbuncle and her kind have won; we don't want to admit it, but they have, so we have to go away to a safe place," his words became soft, like gentle rain after a hurricane, "where the warm sunshine caresses our tired bodies, and there is only Joy and Peace in the pure, delicious air." Some of the women began to sob. "Carbuncle in her gingerbread house will be found out soon enough by the witch-hunters." There was a nearly imperceptible flux in the space-time continuum, but no one noticed. "But until then, we need to retreat, today, this moment, and begin to live." A wry smile appeared on his resplendent face, slipped in between gravity, which sat atop urgency, both of which lay under a bold wilderness of Truth and Righteousness. His stature seemed to enlarge as he walked around the room, and his soothing voice seemed to infuse his friends with hope and equanimity. "It is time to live," he said, as if to defy those who would seek to destroy him. "Now, give me your hands," and he reached out his left hand to Maria and his right hand to Yxta, and they in turn offered their hands to the Teachers, and soon, all of them were holding fast to each other. "You can't get there unless you let go, completely," he whispered passionately, his words piercing through their last layers of rusted resistance.

"I can't," one of the younger women cried, "betray the children."

James sensed that the harmony and tranquility of their growing union trembled and teetered on an unstable foundation. "If you don't let go now, you won't be here to ever help children. Think, think, think, think of the future!" He watched as the woman in question calmed, and he proceeded. "All of you, picture a place in time and space where you want to be and go there, where you are safe and warm and happy—bring your loved ones, too; find a place where no evil person can harm you or see you or bother you, a special place, a Paradise on Earth; go there now, my good friends, go and feel the good, green earth beneath your bare feet and the sultry sun above your smiling face. Feel it now, find it now!"

He explained certain notions and philosophies long forgotten and ignored, and certain methods misunderstood, to all of them, to help them get there to that special land where princely peace reigned.

"No one can ever touch you there," he kindly spoke, seeing their tense faces smooth, their trembling bodies relax; "you'll always be safe there, no matter who, in the outside world, seeks to do you harm."

But then the door opened and Saffron stood under its metallic frame, frowning. "I was drawn here," she said, confused, "as if," she whispered, "I was missing out on something I needed."

Yxta put out her slender hand toward Saffron, her face forgiving, loving, yet despairing.

Saffron looked about the room and saw everyone and intuitively understood that somehow they were nearing a gateway to Paradise; but she looked again to Yxta, and although she felt decency and honor return in herself, she shook her head. Her wet eyes, kindly for that brief second, went back to being hard and cold and dark. She turned her head, quite forgetting why she had come or what she had experienced there, and departed.

"But that is past," Yxta said to her new family. "She is in another spiritual dimension; she no longer has meaning for me. I am free."

"Freedom," James said, urgently, "find it, now. Go! Go! Be there in Paradise with its marbled gateway and forget this bleak place!"

And in a moment, all of the Teachers—except James—were gone, but curiously, they were still physically in the room; but no, there was still one Teacher who stood in the back, immersed in the shadows and leaning against the white walls and aware of things now. "I don't get it, I really don't, James," Mr. McKinley said, sorrowfully, shaking his head. "This isn't supposed to be the way it is; this is all wrong, something is wrong about all of it; I just can't do it, I can't do it, not any of it, not now, no, not anymore," and his head fell to his chest as he took out his classroom keys and laid them on a brown wooden desk and then walked out the door and down the gray cement and out through the open gates to the parking lot and into his car where he turned the key and then drove away, back to his home, where he immediately called the law firm that had offered him a job only eight months ago. He too was free.

The next day Margaret did not have to red light any Teacher on campus.

The Link

But it is not true that every Teacher ascended into the lofty halls of Paradise every day at Amethyst Elementary School; there was one who had agreed to stay behind and be the vigilant guard and intelligence-gatherer on the conquering worm.

Joy Wesley woke up every day with the resolve that the success of the Teachers' campaign for survival rested upon her slender shoulders; she had volunteered for this mission because she was still captive of the idea that teaching was more important than test scores, and that one must not yield to tyrants; when she taught, it was the imparting of exciting knowledge to thirsty minds, revealing her dynamic intellect as she gave them exciting plots to write about, and told stories of ancient battles and heroic men and women and great scientists and great struggles of men and women as they fought for freedom; she always had thousands of books in her room, but the best books in all the world for children—and not those boring books the curriculum coerced upon them: books full of fairy tales and folktales and myths and legends, books full of ancient explorers and their fantastic exploits of derring-do, and novels of fantasy and biographies of great men and women, so that her students just wanted to sit all the day and read; her students engaged in stimulating debates on societal issues and created scientific experiments in her room and read historical documents and heard guest speakers who taught the children about the world they did not yet know; her students read wonderful novels with her and then sang wonderful songs from the movie that was based on the novel and then watched the wonderful movie at

a special time of the year, and they could not have been happier; she had cultural feasts for them during the holidays and
stargazing parties when the nights were warm and clear, and
tasty nutritional root-beer floats for them after hard-fought
soccer battles on the long, green, grassy field; and the students would always understand that they were a family and
that the woman who stood in front of them and spoke so
passionately of the injustices from history and described the
shameful way it used to be for those who were not of the
correct ethnicity or skin color or socioeconomic ranking was
genuine, and a friend.

She had taught for a very long time and for a very long
time she had beaten the best and the worst of principals who
sought to destroy her and deplete her resistance and break her
iron will; but she would not cower or flee and she did fight
and stand tall, and this frightened her principals, because if
they could not bully her, they could not control her.

Therefore, the silent war between Carbuncle and Wesley
continued.

She had to be careful not to betray her comrades, which
is to say, she could not be caught doing what they were
not doing. She had to seemingly be in lockstep with them
at every move from every angle at the proper time and the
proper place, every day of every week without hesitation, or
Mrs. Carbuncle would get wind of the strong scent of defi-
ance and subterfuge that was stronger than the acrid smell of
unchecked Power that emanated from the bloated vision of
her sad, old self.

Joy woke up every morning and exercised, and then ate
a breakfast that would keep her mind lucid and her body
bursting with energy. She was not shy of eating plenty of
protein and whole grains and fruit and vegetables and just
the right amount and proper kind of fat so her inner bodily

workings would be operating on every cylinder and firing every spark plug with maximum efficiency. She would not be undone by a sluggish mind or a weak body.

She was at school early and stayed late. She had nowhere else to be but on this sacred mission; her husband had died, her children were grown and raising their own families; and her children of this generation were here, at this blessed institution, and she would protect them from the day and night stalker, shield them from the mind stalker, the slayer who nightly returned to her chamber of blood and in the morning came back with fresh energy to attempt to destroy all that was proper and fitting. Joy was the lone sentinel, the last soldier to defend the fort, the good citizen who stays behind and wreaks havoc on the enemy so her brethren might escape; and thus she had but a single purpose, and that was to outwit and outlast and dominate this aging, relentless ghoul that had arisen from the crusty, dry crags of the phantom zone wherein unspoken, creepy things dwelt.

She was black of skin and had been cursed and spat on and laughed at and scorned her whole life and she would not yield now to this petty tyranny or any tyranny. She was nearly sixty and she had learned how to survive against an overwhelming enemy who had infinite resources and who seemed disciplined and powerful and incapable of defeat.

"Everyone has an Achilles heel," she would sometimes say, driving to work in the morning as she plotted the activities of the day. "Ask Goliath."

She would get to work and set up her room and talk to her co-conspirators and check the secret systems. Before the bell rang, she would look in the mirror that was glued to the inside of the long cabinet door and she would see an aged face with wrinkles and intense black eyes that burned with an ebullient light and she would secretly smile. "I am ready, old woman," she would say to her absent foe, "come and get me."

And then the bell would ring and the fight was on.

Round one began every morning when Mrs. Carbuncle and Mrs. Willow turned on the red eyes of the invaders and glared into the multiscreen monitors. The administrators watched the Teachers for a solid thirty minutes and compared notes to make sure the Teachers were doing the same thing at the same time in the same way, making sure that the Teachers were moving from one lesson to another with the cold efficiency the administrators had demanded. The two women marveled at the exact precision the Teachers evinced as they glided seamlessly from one subject to the next and delivered the curriculum as directed. They rejoiced that the Teachers taught only those items that would be on the state test, and every day they toasted the idea of high test scores and their possible positions in the highest echelons of the County Education Office or a position at the District Office or as a consultant to other districts; with high test scores, the possibilities of their ascension were limitless, for high test scores were a golden ticket to anywhere in the test-ridden, mad-as-hatters country. They marveled at how even the most outspoken of the Teachers had given in to their relentless pressure. "We will climb to the highest mountaintop," Mrs. Carbuncle would say to Saffron at such times, "on the careers of these pathetic dolts." Saffron would smile and nod her head in full agreement, and now, not even a tiny speck of humanity fell even in secret from her cold and vacuous eyes.

"Why, look at that one," Mrs. Carbuncle said one day, as the two of them sat in their plush, red, high-backed leather chairs, gazing in amusement at the robotic-like movements of their subordinates. It was Joy she spoke of. "Look at her, so proud she used to be, fighting every principal from here

to kingdom come from the moment she became a Teacher."
Black scorn possessed her dry and puffy visage. "And now
she is just as docile and obedient as a newborn lamb." Her
face scrunched up just as if it had been put into a bowl full
of rotting lemons. "Why, the lot of them aren't worth one
plug nickel; and the men, why, those weak sisters," she said,
and Saffron witnessed the pasty-white, flaccid face of her
superior recede and be replaced by a hideous, blotched and
lumpy sand pile of enmity. The words of her Mistress rang
with the authentic shrill of the stalking beast. "And those
men," she recited again, as if her words came now from a
hitherto unknown part of her unconscious mind that reared
its twisted tendrils out of the mire only when its own kind—
sin—neared heavy words, heavy-metal, scorching-hot words
wedded with a seething desire for vengeance, "they have
oppressed women for too long; see how easily they are emas-
culated, how easily they fold and lie down like frightened
children in a thunderstorm; well, this is my school now, my
school to grow, my school to move this way and that, and
they will bend or I will break them." This frosty glee whipped
her words along like a taskmaster to slaves, and Saffron,
though the steel armor of Power had encased her blood and
bone and sinew, still felt a chill like a dull blade caress her
creeping skin. "They will all bow before me or fall before me,
for this school is me." This last statement rose up and came
down and slashed the air with a bloody scythe, chopping
and darting and diving in the breathless air, unbroken in its
fated pattern, the emblem of oppression upon its gleaming
hilt; so it carved, pushed along by the submissive Teachers,
so it shaped, powered by the taciturn Teachers, so it formed
an image of the dying school into the burnished, fiendish
image of its conquering queen. Her voice was seeded with a
choking, grunting appetite for the golden throne of absolute

Power. "They should pledge allegiance to me, for I and this school are one." And she looked up at the lavender ceiling and the white walls and to the screens, and pointed menacingly at the occupants therein, clenching her right fist until it trembled. "And I will crush anyone who gets in my way."

Saffron nodded, and checked to see if her body was still below her throbbing head.

So the two spent their days, like a steamboat captain navigating his way in a dense fog, meandering through the great bulk of notes they took to assure themselves that each Teacher was following the lifeless script to the harshest letter and most oppressive period.

It was a stingingly cold, savagely windy day when the dark dawn was inhaled by the black nostrils of Winter, that the two administrators were observing the Teachers methodically moving through their appointed chores, when an anomaly announced itself on one of the screens and bit Mrs. Carbuncle sharply on her pointy nose. "What in the Sam Hill!" she roared, as sudden as a surfacing whale who blasts her air hole to vent water. She jumped to the screen as if the Teacher in question had committed a violent felony. "Look, look here, something is wrong," she shouted, her face pressed against the black and white monitor. She was shaking with anticipation, and she cursed the fact that the legislators would not allow the sessions in the classrooms to be audio as well as visual. "We have the dirty rebel," she smiled largely, and looked back at her assistant, "finally, we have one of them." And she stood up as does the general who thinks he has the battle won, and then she put out her hand and gripped the air. "Joy is mine." She turned to her subordinate, and said, with great urgency, "Quickly, look at the logs for reading at nine o'clock; the old gal is off," she said, cunningly, "and she is hiding something."

While the exuberant administrators tore into the data sheets, Joy was casually checking the small communications device that sat snugly in her right ear. "The transmission is out," she bemoaned, and tried not to glance at any of the video cameras that sat in each of the four corners of the room, but curiosity led her eyes up to see one of them, and she did not observe a yellow or red light blinking. "She either is not looking or she is plotting," she thought, hesitating at the whiteboard.

Joy was skirting along the edge of a perilous divide between job security and termination with her masterful interpretation of playing the Game; as it was, she was hooked up electronically with a fellow fifth-grade Teacher, so she knew exactly where and what the Teacher was doing all day, but in reality, she was executing her own plans, teaching her own curriculum, putting on the board one version for the intrusive eyes but speaking another for her adoring students. It worked only as long as she seemed to be following her fellow Teachers, and if she could masterfully and seamlessly switch to the feigned lesson if and when any of her prowling administrators came in. But now, the device in her ear that allowed her to hear the other Teacher drone on about a lesson had been off for a good hour, and she had made the mistake of not having the phony lesson plans for that week. All seemed lost.

Any successful guerrilla campaign cannot succeed unless there is collusion between revolutionary and citizen, and indeed, she had the complete loyalty of her students in this matter, a bond forged from all of them being in fourth grade together with her then and now.

"John and Lindsey," she had said at the onset of the malfunction, "keep a lookout for Rosebud." Rosebud was the code name for Mrs. Carbuncle, and the children appreciated the irony of it all after Joy had secretly shown the movie to them that explained the significance of the name. John, a big and mature boy for his age, eagerly took on the role of lookout as he sat near the window and surreptitiously kept his eyes on the outside world, while Lindsey, a passionate lover of knowledge and hater of the new science of test scores, kept a watch on the back door. "Gwen," Joy said, gliding around the room as she faked interest in a ridiculous piece of reading curriculum, "when John gives the word, you know what to do." Gwen did know what to do, and she was a faithful warrior ready to serve.

And then it happened. Mrs. Carbuncle, attempting to break into the room from the back—but temporarily impeded by the old trick of a locked door—compelled Lindsey to give the harsh whisper alarm, which sent Gwen out the door and down the cement walkway.

Mrs. Carbuncle walked in with her ubiquitous clear-plastic clipboard and observation forms, her lips twitching in anticipation as she veered around the room like a tiger that walks among newborn foals. Of course it was too late for her to discover what they had been doing, for the switch had already been made, the switch from the material they were using to the accepted material they were supposed to be using. Mrs. Carbuncle glared at each of the children with revulsion, as if she suspected each of them were in on the ruse.

"Yes," Joy said, in a bland and subservient tone, "how can we better serve you today, Mrs. Carbuncle? Have you any suggestions on this lesson?"

But before Mrs. Carbuncle could respond, the fire alarm blew, and Joy exhaled relief as she and the children walked outside.

Mrs. Carbuncle, always one to strictly follow the rules, reluctantly followed.

Once outside, Joy stood with her fellow guerrilla fighters at her grade level and nudged them toward the light of the present with secret passwords, and they awoke from their insular Paradise, and she explained the technological break-down. Soon, the problem was fixed, all was well, and the Game continued.

Mrs. Carbuncle came into Joy's classroom every hour on the hour for one week but could find no anomaly, and she so relented, for the present, in her assiduous campaign to find out Joy.

But Joy had not taken on the dual role of insider and out-sider for the sole purpose of merely teaching her passion. Two weeks later, one of the lower-grade Teachers lost her control of her inner Paradise and began babbling incoherently about the insensibilities of the curriculum. Saffron found out about it and whisked the woman pell-mell into her office and shut the door, and Margaret's face was now contaminated with an invisible light, a devouring, flickering light that fell in bleak showers upon her glowering countenance, a sobering light drawn from the despicable acts of those interrogators and inquisitors past and present. She felt its flame and flash bathe her face in warmth and sunshine, and she thought it good.

She went about her business of badgering the Innocent, throwing her this way and that as she pulled and tugged and mauled and stomped the poor woman into emotional threads and ashes. "Tell me what you're up to, you stupid girl," she roared at the frightened second-grade Teacher, who wept and shook and looked about for succor. The grand inquisitor low-ered her voice into a vat of saccharine and let it roll about just like a honey-stick in a cotton candy machine. Her face nearly seemed human and her voice saturated with a sickly-sweet, artificial congeniality. "No one to help you now, you've been caught; just confess your sins and Mrs. Carbuncle will not hurt you." But the voice was too far removed from what the Teacher perceived as reality, and this actually served to awaken her from the stagnant borders between her inner Paradise and reality. She shook her head and stared at Mrs. Carbuncle.

Meanwhile, the outside forces, alerted to the crisis by Joy, came back from their inner sanctum and met in stealth. A toxic sweat of fear soaked right through their clothes.

It was James who originated the idea for the rescue. In nearly no time at all, he was in the office, uttering the magic words to Maria and pulling her back from Utopia to give the instructions. "Artemus said this might happen," he thought, watching Maria knock on the prison door of the warden; "let us see if the embedded code works."

"What is it, you meddler?" Mrs. Carbuncle cried from within the torture chamber.

Maria, practicing her best congenial smile, said, "Well, Mrs. Carbuncle, I just wanted to tell you something about your Teacher that might help you…"

Mrs. Carbuncle slammed the door open and charged to the face of the school secretary. Maria never blinked. "What!" she screamed.

"Well, Mrs. Carbuncle," she said, harvesting all the energy in her slender body to hold her composure, "Mrs. Laird is in the middle of a very difficult divorce."

"What? What's this?" she shouted, turning and looking with suspicion at the Teacher who cowered in her chair. "Eh, what is this I hear?" she cried, charging her quarry and slamming the door and planting her sagging visage up to the trembling woman. She turned to Saffron. "Have you heard about this?" and upon receiving a negative reply, looked again to the Teacher. "Well, what of it, you big baby, is it true?" There was, it must be told, a shred of hope in the slashing tone.

The Teacher sat in her web of confusion and her brain began to break through the nebulous haze about her. She began to remember the dialogue about what must be done in the case of discovery by the enemy. Yes, yes, she remembered now, she knew what to do, but she had to be extremely careful. "Yes, yes, it is true," she slowly said, concentrating on remembering to live the lie, be the lie, believe the lie against all opposing forces. "My husband and I are divorcing." And then came the tears, real tears as she manufactured the horrible things her husband was doing to her. She remembered all of it now, all of her instructions from James on how to diffuse the situation if anyone was caught, by gaining the sympathy of the accuser. "Yes, yes, it is all clear, all of it," she thought, and then told Mrs. Carbuncle the entire sordid affair, as if she truly loathed her husband and loathed all men and hated what they were and how they treated all women the world over. She said it with such honesty and fervor and enmity that Mrs. Carbuncle began to lower her resistance to subterfuge.

"But what was all this about Paradise and reality?" Mrs. Carbuncle demanded, hands on her soft-bone hips.

"Well," the poor woman sobbed, crushing the noble image of her beloved husband in her mind to wisps of shrapnel, "Paradise is here, away from that horrible, terrible man," and she broke down and sobbed some more.

Mrs. Carbuncle banged the door open, and cried, "Maria, get the phone number for the Lairds." The phone number quickly retrieved, Mrs. Carbuncle dialed the number and put the phone on speaker and stood in the middle of the carpeted room and waited with a scrutinizing glare that dared the truth to rise up before her.

"Hello?" the male voice answered.

Mrs. Carbuncle nodded to the woman, and the woman commenced. "George, I am calling to tell you I want that divorce. I am going to be strong and not let you bully me into letting you stay."

There was a small pause and then the man on the line, who had answered in such an innocuous tone, began to rip and tear and shout and shriek and spew every variety of unclean comparisons of his wife to the most unwholesome creatures, and then he ripped and tore and spat on women the world over for their vile nature and iciness. He hung up with a blast of vulgarisms and a tirade against all things women.

Mrs. Carbuncle nodded her old head, and approached Mrs. Laird as if the woman were a sister of her own. "You poor child," she said, holding the Teacher's hands.

The ruse had worked, and the danger passed.

Later that night, all of the Teachers assembled at Artemus' house and told him of the desperate tale, how Becky Laird had slipped out of her Paradise and been trapped inside the "chamber of horrors with the beasts from twenty thousand fathoms," and how James had slipped a message to Maria so she could stimulate Becky to remember that the way out was to proffer the fake story of divorce. Luckily, her husband had been at home, and recognizing the code words in his wife's first sentence, played his part masterfully.

It was determined after that night that the Teachers needed to be retrained weekly on the blessed Secret of Paradise. No one disagreed, and no further mistakes were made. The school was still seemingly under the dominance of the cameras, and Saffron, and Mrs. Carbuncle.

A Time to Reap

Amethyst Elementary School became as obedient as a slave chained to an oar.

Teachers smiled and acquiesced to all requests from Mrs. Carbuncle and Mrs. Willow, and said very little except those exact words necessary to explain their actions. Their instruction in the classrooms, as Mrs. Carbuncle saw it, rose considerably.

"Why, those lazy dolts do whatever I say without complaint," she said one day during the fourth year of her reign, to Mrs. Willow, her capable assistant. "I might call them amiable if I didn't know they were up to something." She crinkled her pasty nose. "Are they up to something? Look here, they don't argue anymore, and take abuse willingly; it just isn't natural, it's like they're drugged up on something, like they're in a catatonic stupor; but, oh well, whatever it is they're on, I want to order more," and she rubbed her chin, "but I must admit I do miss watching them grovel like servants to an all-powerful Queen; it just made the day go faster, if you know what I mean."

Mrs. Willow tried to remember something about their odd behavior, but she could not.

"Well, whatever it is," she said, hunching her sagging, bony shoulders, "I'm pleased as punch about it; our test scores will be higher next year, you can bet on that."

The children could attest to her last statement, for all the day long they were taught only those dry, lifeless subjects and skills ad infinitum that were to be on the state test, and consequently, they were bored out of their youthful skulls.

They too eyed their Teachers with suspicion, for they were no longer able to bring their instructors to anger.

And even those students who had often whined about how their Teachers had droned on and on about those subjects they were passionate about, which were not related to state standards, these same students now yearned for such lectures. Why? Because even in their infantile souls, they yearned to hear about long-past civilizations and great heroines and spectacular battles instead of humorless adverbs and syllables and suffixes, and algebraic equations and geometric formulas that were miles above their heads; and they longed for current events and even the lame humor and reminiscences about the old days instead of meaningless, isolated synonyms and antonyms and homonyms, and data sets that numbed their senses; but in the end, in this stale, sterile camp that was now their world at school, they simply wished for information that would stimulate them to listen and learn and feel alive.

The black cloud that had long hung over the school began to sprinkle an unsavory rain that was filled with the seeds of injustice, soaking the naked heads of the Just, but filling the mouths of the Unjust.

A thorny, brownish, bumpy kind of distemper seemed to encircle the bodies of the Just, sealing them in a sugary skin of a cocoon, stealing their passions, their dreams and their hopes. The Just intuitively knew the source of the rain, but their sense of Goodness impeded their seeking retribution against Mrs. Carbuncle.

Assemblies, an integral part of any school, were wiped out. "They won't raise test scores," Margaret said, feeling Power growing in her as if she were pregnant with it. Awards were also not given out. Margaret whined, "How can we give out awards if we don't know how high students' test scores will be until school is out?" Recesses were canceled. "Those lazy children need to work. The little brats can go home and rest up for tomorrow," Margaret sneered, and then uttered, as an aside, "Children smell."

Children see school as a complete dinner, including those foods you need to eat, want to eat, and don't want to eat; now, school to the children was a cold, moldy, raw lump of yellow broccoli.

Students no longer challenged Teachers because Teachers merely smiled at them and went on with their lessons.

Children cried at school. They cried at home.

"I hate school," echoed in every room of the school—on the empty swings it sat, and it stood on the barren blacktop, and it lay on the dewy grass fields and dirt softball fields, and it wept for a future that should have been. These sad words came from students, it seeped out of the minds of the Teachers who knew the Secret, it fell within the glassy, pious tears of the parents.

There was a parade in late October, not a parade to celebrate the children's excitement about Halloween, but a parade to excite the children about raising their state test scores. Banners declared numbers that were supposedly sacred and were a goal to achieve as an overall total for the school for the almighty test. Pride was a creature to be resurrected by students learning skills for the state test, and its name was painted in red, bold letters on white butcher paper by the very accommodating Mrs. Willow; but the festivity was as if in a cemetery, for the students stood blank faced, the Teachers smiled vacuously, and Mrs. Carbuncle issued loud prose to encourage them on toward lofty goals for the sacred test.

The students and Teachers were now as those natives who are conquered by a foreign monarch, to whom they are forced to swear allegiance.

At night, when the campus was deserted except for those custodians who scurried like frightened mice when they saw the Principal coming their way, Margaret would walk through each room, digging through Teachers' desks and grade books, rummaging through students' work and inspecting cabinets; she had to know everything all of them did at all times, for if she did not know, a terrible feeling of anxiety would creep over her, giving her over to nervous fits.

During Winter Recess, when all of the employees of the school were at home with their loved ones, Margaret was on campus, also with her paramour, the school that imbued Power in her.

"No one would dare come here now, the sentimental fools," she remarked one night to herself as she walked into Yxta's classroom for one of her more thorough examinations, "not on their precious Eve." She sat down at Yxta's desk and began to pillage it, when to her utter astonishment she beheld two figures sitting at two students' desks, their hands neatly folded on their laps. "Gadzooks," she cried, feeling her heart pause as it decided whether or not to continue its tiresome rhythmic beating. She stood up, and then gaining her composure when she realized the two were merely children, grew irritated. "Don't you children know school is out? What is the meaning of this?" she demanded. "Are you robbers, eh? Come to rob old Mrs. Carbuncle?" and she picked up a pair of scissors from a desk drawer, waving them menacingly about.

The two children sat with grim expressions upon their cherubic faces. The girl spoke in a voice full of wonder as she turned to look at the boy. "She does need some elementary schooling. Wilhelm was right. She must have skipped essential things."

"Yes," the boy returned, still looking intently at Margaret, "she needs many lessons."

"Do you think," the girl asked, curiously, "she will need all the levels Jacob has suggested?"

The boy squinted hard at the old woman. "I do think it is possible; she is such a human monster."

"What? What?" Margaret shouted. "What are you babbling about? I'll call the police and have you arrested for trespassing." Her thin, pale lips were trembling furiously as she rambled on. "You'll spend the night in juvy, you little brats!" But then she screwed up her small eyes and stared harder. "But don't I know you—aren't you the two juvenile delinquents who grabbed me one day on the playground? Yes, yes, I am sure of it! Oh, you little hoodlums, you'll be written up for this, you'll see!"

The brother and sister stood up, and their ancient peasant clothes became apparent. The girl spoke. "Jacob and Wilhelm said to give you a chance to first repent," and her voice became grave. "Well, old woman, do you repent of your wicked sins?"

"What? Sins!" Margaret exclaimed, becoming increasingly agitated, and then just understanding that she could not physically move her feet prompted her to throw the sharp, black-handled scissors at the children. "I have no sins. Sins are in fairy tales."

"You see, she does not recognize her crimes," the girl said; "she will have to come with us."

"Yes," the boy said, shaking his head, "her journey has only begun."

In the next second forward of measured time, all of them vanished.

Story Time

Margaret was skulking about in the house trying to remember where she had been when she realized this was not her home, but a smaller place adorned in antiquities and smelling strongly of freshly baked cookies and cake. "Eh, what is this? Have I gone mad?" she cried, touching the spongy walls, only to find out they were indeed made of food; and upon tasting a sugary, brown piece of it, she cried, "Egad! It's gingerbread!" She began to walk toward the window, but fell, and soon realized that the wooden pair of crutches leaning against the small, round wooden table was meant for her crippled legs. Thus equipped with the walking aids, she inspected the window, and to her further amazement, discerned that it was made of pure sugar. "How odd," she exclaimed, and then, walking outside, inspected the shingles of the roof, and found them to be made of delicious cake. "This is very strange indeed," she mumbled to herself, walking back into the gingerbread cottage.

Happening upon a mirror, she saw only a hazy picture of herself. "Eh, what is this? My vision has gone bad." Undaunted, she moved closer to the dull, dusty mirror, nearly pressing her wart-tipped nosed against it, and was shocked to see that her small eyes were as red as blood. "Lack of sleep, no doubt," she said, to comfort herself.

Examining the entire place, she found a wire chicken coop outside, but no chickens; many sharp knives, but no food to cut with them except bread. "The poor fool who lived here must have left on account of poverty." Looking into the giant, black iron oven, she saw many burnt bones lying in great heaps. "Ugh! The woman must have eaten like a pig!"

But then a curious event occurred, and she stood still, but not erect, for she was hunched over just like the woman who looks for weeds in her garden; her long, hooked nose tilted up and she could smell something that, to her, had the strong odor of succulent meat. In her mind, this ripe scent built a picture of human beings, and her mouth watered at the thought of them cooking in the iron stove. "Strange that I fancy eating people, as much as I do detest them; I do suppose that I might as well eat them if I have no use for them."

It wasn't until a good hour later that she heard voices outside her gingerbread house, and all the while the yearning for tasty, salty flesh had aroused in her a healthy appetite.

"Eh, what's this?" she whispered to herself, observing a young boy eating parts of her roof, and a young girl eating portions of her sugary window. She rubbed her knotted, crooked hands together and, standing by the door, she said, in a sweet voice,

"Nibble, nibble, little mouse, who is nibbling at my house?"

A reply soon came from the children,

"The wind on high, the child of the sky."

After deliberating about the children, and devising a plan to entrap them, she opened the door, introduced herself, invited them in, fed them, and prepared beds for them so they might stay the night.

In the morning, Margaret seized the boy, took him outside to the wire chicken coop with the grated door and locked him therein. Coming back to the girl, she said, harshly, "Get up, you lazybones, and fetch some water so you may cook for Hansel. He needs to be good and fat before I eat him."

Gretel cried but did what the old witch ordered, for she was very much afraid of her.

Margaret made sure Hansel ate the best of everything so he might get good and fat, while poor Gretel ate only crab shells. Every morning the old witch asked Hansel to stick out his finger to see how fat he was becoming, but he always put out a little bone, and the old witch was deceived because of her poor eyesight, and thought it was his finger.

"That boy must have worms." Margaret scowled at Gretel, and went about her business, scolding her for praying to God for help. Then, later that night, she said, so sweetly that the child's innermost alarm system was on high alert, "I am going to bake bread, honey child—why don't you crawl inside the oven to see if it is hot enough?" But seeing Gretel hesitate, she growled, and pushed the frightened girl toward the stove as the yellow flames roared inside it. Of course, the old witch meant to push Gretel inside and roast her and eat her. And as Gretel stood in front of the hot stove, Margaret had the most curious thoughts.

"It is as if," she mused, "I have the freedom to not kill the children...but I do love children," she fretted. "I do," and she giggled with a deep pleasure within her black heart, "but with a little salt and pepper. Oh, fie; this is who I am; I hate people, and children, who are, unfortunately, people, I hate most of all—O, I think I hate men even more! But seeing that there are none of them around, I will have my meal of these two ragamuffins." She once more resolved to push Gretel inside the oven, but the child complained that she was ignorant about how to check if the stove was hot enough.

"Stupid goose," the old witch scolded her and, coming to the oven, she put her round head inside it, "see?"

But then Gretel pushed Margaret inside the iron oven and shut the black door with a loud clang.

The sizzling flames began to devour Margaret's screaming, sizzling flesh, and as she cried in horror and agony and banged weakly on the locked iron door, terrorized voices echoed in her ears. "Old witch," she heard, and it seemed as if the charred bones of the child victims were singing a rueful choir of repentance to her, "pray, seek forgiveness for your sins from almighty God; repent, Margaret, for your wicked heart."

Pain chewed into her brain as the scorching flames fried her and baked her and ate her alive. Margaret screamed until her lungs burst and were consumed by her own noxious fumes, and then she screamed inside her maniacal mind, cussing and cursing Hansel and Gretel.

The chorus of children's voices did not relent. "Repent, ye sinner, for your wicked deeds," the wailing voices thundered inside the tight cube of orange-red conflagration.

"Never!" Margaret hollered in her frenzied mind as her body burned into smoked, burnt ruins. "I hate children," she screamed, as her body smoldered in the sooty ashes. Her consciousness survived the gruesome fire, and she felt the unfettered agony of torment engulf her physical fury for hours. She went mad even as her corpse lay in a twisted, black, charred heap, her mind insane with incoherent, babbling streams of verbal drooling; yet, repent she would not.

Then it all seemed a surreal dream because she was once more standing in Yxta's room, looking suspiciously at the two children who sat solemnly at their desks. Her shaking body was gasping for the stark air of reality, her red face was aghast, her small eyes wide, her hands held up in the air as if to grab onto something tangible. In an hour, she managed to let words crawl out of her now-twitching mouth. "You brats," she muttered, "you little monsters. It was you."

Hansel looked at her rather stoically. "But have you learned anything?"

"I will say she has not," Gretel said, frowning, looking at her brother. "She would have been just happy to push me right into that awful stove," and turning toward Margaret, she continued, "Don't you know it's wrong to cook children and eat them?"

"Why, you vile creatures! Accuse me of wrongdoing? You burned me alive! I'll get you," she shouted, but alas, her feet were still wedded to the blue carpet.

"Unlike many others, she has accepted it as reality," Gretel said, plainly, "but it's also obvious, Hansel, that she still blames others and is blind to her own sins."

"Well, back you go, you old goat," Gretel said, in earnest, "unless, of course, you have decided to repent?"

"Never!" Margaret exclaimed, holding her head up high.

Margaret remembered seeing the two Germanic adolescents waving goodbye to her even as she stood in the gingerbread house once more, and once more, when all was said and done and she had lived the adventure again, she was roasting away in the iron stove, swearing and threatening those whom she perceived to be her two oppressors.

And once again she stood in Yxta's room, her face blanched with fear, her tired body quaking as she stared at the two placid-looking children. "If you're trying to make me say 'uncle,' I won't do it!" she shouted, shaking her fist at them.

Hansel's kind face reflected his disappointment. "Is there not one morsel of regret about the way you have treated people?"

"Admit wrong and you will not go to Level Two," Gretel said, sweetly. "Is there no reflection at all on how you treat people?"

"Hogwash!" Margaret yelled. "We are what we are, so we do what we do; who is to say what is right or wrong? You want me to confess to a crime I haven't committed. But you? Ha! You're tyrants, and should be hung from a tree and be eaten by wolves."

"Careful," Gretel said, her voice dark and savage, "a wish given is a wish taken. You must take it back."

"Ho, ho! I have found you out! I get a wish, too! Well, I wish that the both of you are hung from a tree until your eyeballs bulge out from the hot sun and the insects eat you and worms are coming out of your eyes, and then you fall to the ground and are eaten by wolves—no, dogs; wolves aren't around here, so I'll be practical," and then she screamed in a guttural rage, her face purple with wrath, "and may it never end!"

Hansel stared hard at Margaret, his face long and lean. "Level Two, now, for you, you bad woman; yet, now you will become a person of a higher status so you might achieve a greater good; and you will remember everything if you want to. If you do good, old woman, you will live."

The violent image of Margaret holding out her hands toward them in a defiant gesture faded into a swirling mist.

"I am young and beautiful again," she cried, prancing about the exquisite palace room with its marble statues and ruby-studded gold cups, "and I am rich!" She soon realized who she was. "Queen! Queen of an entire country!" She danced around the vases of burnished bronze and stamped on the jade steps that led to her room. Presently, she realized, much to her vexation, that she was the wife of a king—as queens often are—and from that day onward, she plotted to have him murdered, as queens sometimes do; but, alas, she was always unsuccessful.

"The magic of the little brats is weaker than mine," Margaret murmured to herself one day, as she watched fragrant water poured over her smooth hands by her handmaiden; and as she watched rose petals placed carefully upon her silken pillow by another servant, she said, "I am home," and she laughed inside her swirling thoughts.

She lay in bed, musing upon her fate. "Those two loathsome brats wait for me to do evil, but I won't; I am not a bad person. I am a born leader, and leaders do things that must be done, which seem evil." The more she dwelt upon it, the quicker she became frustrated, and she had a way of assuaging all such fits of anxiety. "Bah!" she shouted, and instantly she felt relieved.

The next day she went about her kingdom looking to do noble acts, but found none to do. "Squalor everywhere! These people wouldn't understand a good deed done to them! What am I supposed to do, tell them not to be ignorant peasants who live in horrible filth in their own disgusting waste? Tell them not to obey me? Why, these imbeciles need me!"

Everywhere she went in her golden and purple-velvet carriage, she saw rotting disease, peasants mangled from wars and accidents, decaying houses constructed from mud and timber and peasant blood and sweat. Their dire faces radiated joy when she came up to them.

"The poor ignorant masses need rulers," she mused, watching a toothless, emaciated young woman holding a baby that had bedsores all over its frail body. "They look to us for hope and direction; without me they would die! I give them life, a reason to live!"

She sat in her royal castle, counting her marvelous treasures, convincing herself that a good deed for the masses would be to not raise their taxes nor issue harsher penalties for their crimes.

Daily, her own people petitioned her to reduce sentences sent down upon their loved ones by her harsh courts.

"My good, gracious Queen," one man began as he prostrated himself before her, "I am but a poor cobbler, and have no money; but, I pray thee, O great and merciful Queen, my poor boy is in the dungeons for stealing a cup of grain from the local granary, and…"

"Stop!" the Queen shouted. "The boy is guilty?" and when she saw the bald old man slowly nod his head, she smirked. "You dare take my precious time with your whining?" She had the man condemned to the dungeons, one cell from his son. "Misery loves company," she said later to one of her female courtiers. "You may quote me on that; let it be known that the Queen is not only beautiful but full of wit, too."

A decree was sent out the next day to her royal guards, and it read, "Disguise yourselves as peasants and complain about the Queen and her laws, and carefully mark down the names of those who say one word against her Royal Highness, even in jest; so that later, those guilty parties should taste the whip and the stench of the gallows for their treason!"

A month hence, after her official edict had been executed by her officials and soldiers, she felt an insatiable appetite to scourge the land of all who opposed her. She imposed the cruelest taxes, the longest jail sentences, claimed more lands of nobles and peasants, and when it was all said and done, she felt truly invincible.

"Those foolish children," she said one day to herself as she admired her rare beauty in her silver mirror, "they have not condemned me but freed me to be who I truly am! I tell you, ruling a kingdom is no different from ruling a school." But she often began to believe that her existence at Amethyst Elementary had been but a bad dream, and that the two children were part of that distant nightmare. "My beauty is so exquisite," she said to herself, admiring her long, thick, black hair and her high, red cheekbones and her thick, ruby-colored lips. "Is there another so rare, eh? Well, what say ye, Mirror?" and then she was compelled to ask it, as if she were in trance,

"Mirror, Mirror, on the wall,
Who is the fairest of them all?"

And the mirror responded, much to her amazement,

"Queen, you are the fairest of them all."

Flushed with pride at the mirror's proclamation, Margaret closed her eyes. "This magical mirror hath spoken the truth!"

Immediately, she sent for the royal artist and had him begin to paint her portrait. "But I want this painting to be in the home of all my subjects; do what you must, hire apprentices, but get it done or lose your head."

A royal edict went out a year later, that every citizen must have the portrait of the Queen hanging in their house or risk imprisonment; and if a soldier or official of the court were to find the painting not the highest object on the walls, or having a speck of dirt, then a visit to the dungeons was guaranteed for the guilty citizen.

The Queen tested the magic of the mirror often, but found, to her dismay, that it could answer only one question, regarding her beauty. The mirror had been silent on all other questions by the Queen, such as, "Which courtiers are team players? Is the court jester really funny? Which of my adjutants would die for me?" By now, the Queen had completely forgotten who she had once been.

Alas, when the Queen needed her monolithic ego inflated one cubic inch more, she would address the mirror again and again, if only to hear the same, reassuring, monotonous chant.

During the second year of her present reign, on a pleasant, warm Summer eve, when the light, wispy cirrus clouds drifted lazily across an azure sky, when the multihued flowers, sitting in branched clusters, opened their scented, velvety buds, and when the hope of living was renewed, the Queen stood before the dull mirror and asked the question she had asked it thousands of times before,

"Mirror, Mirror, on the wall,

who is the fairest of them all?"

Expecting the same answer, she smiled, but then, to her utter shock, a different answer came back,

"Queen, you are still fair,
but Snow White is the most beautiful of all."

Now, Snow White was known to the Queen, for the little girl was her stepdaughter, and upon hearing this proclamation from the mirror, she had to believe what it said, for to disbelieve it would be to dismiss the mirror's claim that the Queen had been the fairest in the land until now. However, the Queen was overwrought with jealousy, and rage appeared like red blisters upon her boiling brain.

"Snow White must die," she vowed, that very second, and the next day she hired a huntsman to take Snow White out to the woods and kill her; but as it was, once out in the deep woods, the huntsman took pity on Snow White and let her go.

Instead, the huntsman killed a boar, cut out its liver and lungs, and took it back to the Queen as proof that Snow White was dead. The Queen was so delighted that she ordered the cook to boil and salt the lungs and liver, and she promptly ate the delectable organs. "It seems I have an appetite for children, after all," she giggled to herself.

The Queen, with the fresh taste of the organs' meat still upon her greasy lips, stood in front of her enchanted mirror and asked it the same question as always, but now received more information than before: not only that Snow White lived but where she lived and with whom. She soon devised a plan to murder Snow White herself and keep the deed from her husband, the King. "I shall disguise myself as an old woman peddler," she said to herself, "and use my cunning to murder this annoying little brat."

So, she dressed herself up as an old peddler woman and journeyed into the forest and across the hills until she reached the pleasant little cottage of the seven Dwarves. She knocked on the door and said in her most appealing voice, "Wares for sale, fine wares for sale!"

But Snow White, having been admonished by the Dwarves about strangers, said, "I mustn't let anyone in; it is not safe, the Dwarves told me so."

"If you will only look at these beautiful laces and bobbins of all colors I have, you will certainly want one."

And so Snow White opened the door a bit to see the harmless-looking old woman who held the yellow basket with the fine laces and bobbins in it, and so, her heart and mind, so full of innocence and trust for the world, opened the door and allowed the woman in and offered her some tea and biscuits, to which the woman, who looked about the place, nervously agreed. "Are you so poor that you must travel the long roads just to sell these trinkets?" Snow White asked. "I will buy one of these pretty combs, if only to help you," and she held the woman's hand as they sat at the small table together. "The Dwarves have told me to watch out for strangers, but I must help those in need, and not only those I know; the Dwarves helped me, and I was but a stranger to them."

"Bah," the Queen thought, "what a foolish child! Wasting her money on a stranger! What good is that! What good will it do her or anyone?" But then she said, aloud, "Why, missy, your stays are so badly laced! Let me lace them up with my pretty new laces!" And she proceeded to lace up Snow White so tightly that the young girl soon stopped breathing, and fell down as if one dead. "There, finally," the Queen said, rubbing her chin, "you are dead now, you ridiculous child," and she quickly left the cottage and crept away into the forest and hills, only to be violently molested by the animals of the forest whom Snow White cared for and loved.

That night, the Dwarves came back and found Snowdrop—for that was what they called her—on the floor, as if dead; but behold, as they took out the new laces, they found that she was only unconscious and soon awake; and then she told her seven protectors about the peddler woman, and they immediately declared that the old woman was none other than the Queen herself, and that Snowdrop should not open the door to anyone while they were gone.

The Queen went home and consulted the mirror and found once again to her chagrin that Snow White was still alive, and so she determined to once more set out in disguise, but this time in a different dress, to the cottage of the Dwarves and do away with the child.

"Wares for sale, fine wares for sale," she said, as she once again stood outside the small cottage that sat in front of a silvery, bubbling brook.

"I must not open the door to anyone," Snow White said; "the Dwarves have told me so, and they are very wise men, indeed."

"Do you not have pity for a poor woman who honestly tries to make a living? Would you have me a criminal instead, stealing, or being a beggar woman in the streets?"

Snow White, her heart suffused with pride and love for succor, opened the door, allowed the woman in, and poured her tea and prepared for her a small cake, with sweet berry jam she herself had crushed and jarred only that morning. "How can I turn away from helping those in need, even when I am in danger?" Snow White said to the old peddler woman. "I know I must help those in need; we are here to help each other. This is what the wise Dwarves have taught me. Is this not so, peddler woman?"

"Yes, yes, I suppose so," the woman replied, quickly, as if she had never heard such a philosophy expounded aloud.

"And who have you helped in your life? You seem so kind and giving, I am sure you have helped many."

The old peddler woman rubbed her bare chin, and thought for a moment, but could not think of anyone. O phooey, she cried in her thoughts, the girl dies. "Try this beautiful comb, my dear," she said, aloud, "it will make your long and thick hair even prettier." And she watched in ecstasy as Snow White put the poisoned comb in her own hair and then promptly dropped down senseless. The Queen stood over the fallen body of her nemesis, and growled, as if she were a panther standing over a fallen prey, "Dead, finally, you foolish, ridiculous, trusting girl," and she turned and left the cottage, sneaking away into the hills just as does the snake after a kill; but once more, the animals of the forest came after her, the owl and the dove and the deer and the fox, howling and screeching and attacking her and driving her onward.

That night, the seven Dwarves came home and found poor Snowdrop seemingly dead upon the wooden floor, but after they pulled out the poisoned comb, they revived her, and admonished her once more to never allow anyone in while they were away.

Once again, the Queen consulted her mirror, only to find, to her horror, that Snow White lived still. She cursed the luck of the girl, and determined to bring the youth to her death the next day; thus emboldened, she dressed as a peasant's wife, and set out to the cottage in the morning. Upon arriving, she announced herself and held up a straw basket of fine, ruby-red apples for sale.

Snow White put her head outside the window. "I must not allow anyone in—the kindly Dwarves have told me so; two times before I was betrayed by a woman who was not who she was supposed to be, and I must not allow a third time, or I might surely die."

"But what have you to fear from me, my pretty girl?" the peasant woman said, in her most appealing voice. "Do you fear these apples? Surely, no one has ever died from eating one."

"I suppose you are right," Snow White said, and allowed the woman inside the cottage, and then poured the woman some tea and offered her bread, with fresh marmalade jam that she had made herself that very morning. "The wise Dwarves have told me it is better to be safe than trust anyone, but if they had done thusly, where would I be? They helped me when I was poor and afraid. Have they not given me their home to live in, and their fidelity and protection from all harm?"

"Well, I suppose so," replied the peasant woman, who really did not seem to care.

"Then you too are welcome to our home if you need rest or succor, for we are all here to help each other, for that is what the Dwarves have taught me, and I know it now to be a greater Truth."

The peasant woman sat and thought about the words of this darling child, and she sucked them into her hot nostrils and expelled them out with her rancid breath. "Poppycock," she cried inside, "what a fool! This world is full of trouble, and the only way to stay alive is to trust no one but yourself and help no one but yourself; this is the way of the world, and the way of me!" And she thought of her role as queen and her power and her potential to effect change, but she booed it right out of her thoughts. "Bah! I am here for me, to

serve myself and those like me! I am a queen because of who
I am, and this," and she looked with disgust at her enemy,
"pathetic child will die because she is gullible to the point of
absurdity and stupidity. Now, die, you trusting dolt!" And
then she said aloud, with a sweet and pleasing voice, "Here,
take an apple, it is yours to keep; pay me nothing, for you
have inspired me to do a good deed."

Snow White, encouraged by the apparent generosity of
the woman, reached out to grab the delicious-looking apple,
but hesitated.

"Do you think it poisoned? You do not trust me?" the
peasant woman muttered, nearly weeping. Snow White protested innocence, but yielded to the wisdom of the Dwarves
and declared that she must still be cautious. "Well, I will
show you it is safe," the woman said, and plainly took a large
bite out of one side of the apple and chewed it and swallowed
it right away. Snow White, thus inspired, took the apple and
took a bite out of the other side; but alas, the side of the apple
she chose was poisoned, and this time she fell down, dead.

The Queen looked at the girl in whom she saw all things
that she despised. "You little fool! You trust everyone—you
think that we are here to help each other; well, where are
you now, you fool! If you were more like me, you would be
alive! You would know that to serve oneself is the greatest act
one can do, and the greatest faith you can achieve; it is self,
not others, foolish, foolish girl, that wins the day. So," she
cried, and she swept up her arms and raised them on high,
"now you will die, and even your precious and wise Dwarves
will not save thee," and she slunk away out of the door and
into the hills, just as a murderer does who wears the veil of
wickedness and who serves the doctrines and creeds of darkness; and again, the animals of the forest came upon her and

scolded her and screamed and screeched and howled at her until she was battered and bruised and nearly driven mad.

That night, the Dwarves came home and found Snowdrop upon the floor, and immediately they put her upon a table of polished wood and combed her beautiful black hair and washed her face with water and wine, but alas, they could not revive her, and so they bewailed her death. So they took her and laid her upon a bier and they all mourned for her three whole days; but when it came time to bury her, they gazed upon her rosy cheeks and her fresh face, and decided they could not bury her in the cold ground; instead, they built a glass coffin and wrote with golden letters upon it that she was the daughter of a king; and they set the coffin among the hills and forest and they determined that one of them would always safeguard it. And the animals of the forest and the air came to mourn her too, the owl and the dove and the raven and the deer, and many more.

Thus did Snowdrop lie in her glass coffin for a very long time, and still it looked as though she was only asleep, for her skin was as white as snow and her lips as red as blood and her hair as black as ebony. Then one day a young prince came by and saw the coffin and read the words that were written upon it, and he begged the Dwarves that he might take the coffin to his palace; but the Dwarves would not let Snowdrop go, saying they would not part with her for all the gold on Earth. Yet, the Prince continued to implore them, and presently, the Dwarves relented, and when the glass coffin was removed, behold, a piece of the poisoned apple that was still lodged in Snowdrop's throat came out, and she awoke. The Prince declared his love for her and asked her to be his wife, and she assented, and then asked the Dwarves to accompany her to the palace to live the life they had earned with their

Goodness; but the Dwarves merely said that what they had done for Snowdrop was a commandment from God, and that they would stay in their pleasant cottage. Snowdrop thanked them and promised to return to them often, and then she and her young Prince rode away together toward his royal palace.

And where was the Queen during this time? Well, she had come home after poisoning Snow White and, upon consulting the mirror and learning that Snow White was dead and that she, the Queen, was the loveliest in the land, she rejoiced and danced about her ornate boudoir. "The foolish girl, the stupid goose," she said, "she died trusting people; three times she was fooled, and the third time was the charm. Ho! If she had never trusted anyone, she would be alive today," and she rubbed her chin, "perhaps in a dungeon somewhere, but alive, yet," and she rejoiced once more.

And now, she felt unencumbered, like a lioness who has been dragging heavy chains about her massive body, and she set to carving out the kingdom in her own image.

Her first royal decree demanded that her subjects refer to her from a variety of titles, such as "The Great Gift," or "Queen of the World," or "The Most Beautiful Person in Existence." She began to round up all women who even approached a level of modest beauty, and she had them stashed in dungeons and tortured and beaten and then displayed in stocks in full public view until any woman anywhere near modestly beautiful either ran pell-mell to the hills or covered her face in public so that only her eyes showed; but then a rumor went about that young women who purposely disfigured the fine symmetry of their faces were rewarded handsomely by the Queen, and so many young women began to disfigure their comely faces. After a few months of this gruesome practice, the Queen let it be known that the reward for such maidens was the life of the spinster, and that they would be better off for it, too.

But this was not enough for the Queen, and she began to round up any young maiden who displayed a shapely figure, and she had them thrown into her increasingly expanding prison system (a system that now had so many guards that they formed a very powerful league and oftentimes were the only citizens who were able to obtain concessions from the Queen), and there the maidens were flogged and beaten and tortured and starved until their horribly altered and emaciated bodies were hoisted up into the wooden stocks and displayed for all to see; and so, every maiden who had a shapely figure either ran pell-mell to the hills or began to starve herself or eat so much food that her body became grossly distorted, but their lives were saved, and the Queen appeased, too.

But even still, the Queen was not satisfied, for she did not like what the peasants said about things. "Oh, you know, things!" the Queen cried to her new court jester. "Oh, they may say that a flower is pretty, but how do I know they do not mean it about someone else, eh? Secrets, secrets—I do not like such things—secrets, secrets," she murmured, staring at her curious clown, "I will not have them, anymore."

Therefore, to the surprise of no one in her kingdom, a new edict was sent forth that proclaimed that the word "pretty" was banned, whether it be the spoken word or in print. It is not so different, some of the people whispered to each other, it is only one word, we can live with that; yes, they might have, until the Queen heard a member of her royal court cautiously describe a golden sunset as beautiful, and so, that grand and joyous word "beautiful" was banned the next day;

and the next day after that, the local Professor of Literature went and hid the only known thesaurus in all the land.

But the Queen was not satisfied, no, she was not satisfied with towering over the people due to her riches and power and beauty only, so she amassed an army of spies and sent them out into the villages and even into the palaces of the aristocrats and her royal court and ministers, and there they were to listen and write down any complaint these people made against her; and when all was said and done, when the spies came back and the Queen had reviewed their written word, she summoned those accused and had them thrown into her ever-expanding prison system (the guards had become even more powerful now, and were fast becoming like nobles), and there they were flogged and beaten and starved; but this was not enough, and the Queen decided that these people, some of whom she knew to be dangerous because of their intellect, should think kindly of her, so she had built a monstrous complex wherein these political prisoners might be reeducated by expert manipulators of the mind, and their sympathies toward the Queen redirected.

But this was not enough, for there were still people who opposed her, as she saw it, if not openly, then by their title or riches or perceived power; thus, she put out a decree that no one should own more wealth than the commonest peasant, and so she confiscated all the wealth of the nobles and aristocrats and all the land of the people, and she declared that the state now owned the wealth and the land, and that when the people needed things—but only those items the Queen deemed appropriate—she would give them to the people. "After all," she remarked to the court jester, "all of us are equal—well, all ordinary people are equal—and when one person has more than another, it brings jealousy," and then she had screamed, and her face became scarlet with rage, just as if someone had melted a sack of purple and black beets and thrown the boiling liquid onto her twitching visage, "and I won't have it!"

The court jester, perplexed by her sudden descent into anger, said, sans prior engagement with his foolish brain, "Madame Queen, the Greatest Human Being Ever to Walk the Earth and Who is More Beautiful than Anyone in Human History."

"Go on," she said, admiring his exact reciting of one of her many titles, her vanity stroked and lathered now by this flattery.

"I worry when you become so upset," and he cocked his head so that his tall blue and green silk hat fell over to one side. "Have you heard of anger-management therapy?"

"Eh? What's this? What is that you say, you dunderhead?" she exclaimed, her expanding ego beginning to deflate, like a big, round balloon pricked.

He produced a book from under the loose folds of his red and blue, oversized shirt. "I have been reading about something called 'Intermittent Explosive Disorder,' you see," and the fool actually began to approach her, which was, of course, outlawed, for one could approach the Queen only with her consent (she had especially enjoyed making the rich and powerful citizens of her kingdom, when they neared her, crawl on their knees and make sounds like a baby, or grovel before her and bark like a dog or meow like a cat or waddle like a duck), "I am beginning to believe that…"

"Outrageous!" the Queen screamed.

"There it goes again," he said, frowning, "very strange."

The jester was immediately arrested and thrown into prison. The next day an edict went out that all scholarly books relating to human emotions must be turned in, and that any citizen caught with such books would be arrested and thrown into prison; but when only four books arrived at the chief village collection sites during the next week, an edict was then put forth that banned the owning of all books. Naturally, the Teachers in the kingdom protested, and yes, they were then arrested and thrown into prison—but before that, each of them was made to walk around town while wearing a tall, pointy dunce cap made of a thick and gooey, fresh, brown manure, past townspeople who collected rotten eggs and overripe tomatoes at "Pound the Teacher and Win a Prize" centers and threw them at their former taskmasters who were wearing a chain collar that had a thick rope attached to it, which led to a very mischievous monkey who had on a cute little professor's satin purple robe and big, black horn-rimmed spectacles as he scampered around, tugging on the short tether and chattering with glee behind one of the Queen's social monitors, who made sure the prisoner could not wipe their face or evade a thrown object; now, it must be said that whenever the Queen's subjects were sent to the rack and tortured, she never once visited them, but this time she made an exception; and when she did arrive, she found it most pleasurable, she said, to have a "hands-on experience" with these very articulate but wailing Teachers. She always walked away from these sessions with a broad grin on her very handsome countenance.

But this was not enough for the Queen, for she still felt that the people were not properly worshipping her, so she decided that the priests in the village should mention her in their services as "The Queen Chosen by God" or "The Best Queen in the World." But even this did not satisfy her, for her spies found that the priests were not sincere in the pronouncement of these titles, so the Queen had the priests arrested, and when the people protested, she had them arrested too, and thrown into the ever-expanding prison system (where the guards had become so powerful they were like nobles and aristocrats now, they being the only group— along with the army—who curried favor with their ruler), where they were tortured and flogged and beaten, and oftentimes placed into the reeducation system.

But still, even though all her political enemies and female rivals were dust and ashes underneath her feet, and even though she owned all the wealth and all the land, and even though the people never overtly spoke ill of her, she was not satisfied. "It is as if," she said one day to the court jester, "they are thinking bad thoughts about me but won't say them aloud; if only I could get into their infantile brains and find out! Well, if I cannot do that," she said, staring at the silly countenance upon her multicolored clown, "I will not allow the slightest disturbance to even trickle out..." The clown dropped his silly frown and stood upright and bore a hard frown, for which he was promptly arrested and thrown into prison.

A new edict went out the next day. "Frowns will no longer be tolerated in this happy kingdom." But the people, naturally fraught with frowns as they beheld this new proclamation on the fine, white scrolls that were nailed to the community bulletin boards (every citizen had to, upon arising, rush out to these ubiquitous and colossal wooden boards and check for every new proclamation, and any citizen not seen doing so was arrested and thrown into prison); well, these people were, well, they were soon arrested and thrown into prison. "There will be no more frowns!" the edict reaffirmed the next day. "People will generally smile as much as possible, and smile when the name of Queen is spoken." And the people soon learned, and so the edict was obeyed.

The next day, the Queen mandated that all people would no longer be able to live by themselves, but with Queen-appointed "social monitors," formerly known as spies, or, as the people called them, the QSs, or Queen's Spies, and that these monitors would accompany the people everywhere and write down any infraction of the new edicts.

Well, the Queen seemed satisfied for a while, until she heard that some of the social monitors were accepting bribes from the families they lived with, and that other monitors were evincing affection and sympathy for the people they lived with. "Outrageous!" the Queen cried, slapping her royal diamond-ruby-jade-encrusted scepter against her golden throne. "There will be no sympathy in this kingdom unless it is for me! Loyalty to me and to me only—that is the way it must be with queens!" And so, by another royal edict, she mandated that all social monitors would also have spies watching them, and any monitor violating any edict would be thrown into the ever-expanding prison system (where the guards, who were so powerful and rich now, had hired people to take their places while they basked in luxury in their own mansions).

The Queen was now satisfied, but this did not last long. "What is wrong with me," she said aloud one day to her newest court jester, who had trouble remembering the edicts he must not violate, "why don't I have an appetite for killing? Any fool knows that a Queen must scourge the land of traitors and criminals on occasion, or the people will think her weak!" She looked to the jester. "Well, fool, why didn't you think of that! What good are you if you don't have my best interests at heart! Now, now," she murmured, rubbing her pointy, white chin, "how to do it, how to do it; let us see, let us think on it for a while, and I will soon do it, a while." And so she ruminated about it a while, and came back to her throne of pure gold and her scepter of rare jewels. "I do believe I have it: I shall boil them in oil." She frowned. "But as I say it, it sounds so common." She walked around the cowering court jester. "I could dunk them in great tanks of icy water until they confessed their crimes and then drown them anyway—playing fair is for mortals; yes, yes, that might suffice; or I could always chop off their heads, or place delicious food before them and starve them to death." She frowned even harder. "So many choices, so many different directions give one a headache." She looked to the jester. "You, buffoon, tell me a joke or a riddle, and I might reward you—with your life," and she howled as does the mighty tsunami as it descends upon the tiny island.

The jester gulped and looked at her, desperately attempting not to portray fear, which she had already outlawed for any subject in her presence, or to show anxiety, which she too had outlawed, or procrastination—yes, yes, she had outlawed that too, and had had many amusing moments listening to people, as they attempted to shield their true thoughts from her, issue forth the most ridiculous answers imaginable in responding to her questions. "Well, your Highness, I do have a riddle." She smiled, and he too smiled, and then cleared his throat. "What comes on the morrow and brings you sorrow?"

"Yes, curious, a curious riddle," she said, walking around the trembling jester, which, of course—trembling near royalty—was a serious offense; "let us see—the wind, the rain, a drought, a famine, an invading army?" But to every answer he said no, and she soon grew perplexed at his laughing and dancing and outward signs of cockiness (yes, it is true—"outward signs of cockiness" near the Queen were outlawed).

"That is enough, you popinjay! I will issue another edict tomorrow, that every answer I give is the correct one—for I am infallible; after all, God chose me," and she looked with disgust at the shrinking jester, "and not you, you miserable bug! Now, tell me the answer that I already know—and it had better be an answer worthy of my precious time that you have wasted—or off to prison you will go."

He was nearly in a fetal position, whimpering like a kicked dog, when he, his hand still covering his eyes, said, in a feeble voice, "The King comes home."

The Queen gasped. "You lie," she screamed, kicking the poor wretch, "how would a worthless peasant such as yourself know such weighty matters?"

The jester, emboldened that she had not yet caused him to be hauled away, said, mildly now, "Everyone knows it, but since you outlawed secrets—and secrets that cause you sorrow—well…"

The Queen, enraged now beyond all senses, summoned all of her royal court and demanded they give her news on the return of the King; all of them knew it, and all of them had been afraid to tell her; and so, all them were arrested and thrown into the ever-expanding prisons (where the new guards of the old guards were too becoming so powerful that they had formed their own group and were treated with caution and respect by the Queen), and beaten and tortured and slated to be sent to the giant reeducation camps.

Well, her husband, the King, finally returned after several years away fighting foreign armies, only to find that his Queen had disobeyed his orders, and had, in fact, persecuted the citizens more than ever. For days the King mused upon what to do with her, until, finally, the answer came to him when a neighboring king's son told him how he had rescued

Snow White from a state of purgatory as she rested in a glass coffin that had rested on a mountaintop that had been guarded by seven kindly, devoted Dwarves, and how the Queen had thrice attempted to kill Snow White.

That night, while the Queen stood before the enchanted mirror and heard it say once more that Snow White was indeed alive and more beautiful than she, the King stepped out from the dark shadows.

"Only your wickedness exceeds your beauty," the King said, gravely, "and tomorrow you shall attend the wedding of the young Prince and my daughter, Snow White, whom you tried to kill but whose Goodness saved her," and he departed, brokenhearted.

"Men," the Queen grumbled, "they have always been the source of my problems." She began to reflect upon her life, and it seemed as if she had once held a less noble station in life. "But how could that be? Born a queen, die a queen!"

The next day, she attended the joyous wedding of Snow White and the Prince, but as soon as she walked into the great hall with all its merriment and brightly colored ornaments, clad in her magnificent purple gown and crown jewels, the King greeted her with a kiss, which she took on her cheek. She was angry with him, and had decided not to speak to him for an extended period of time. "He will forgive me soon enough," she comforted herself. "Queens do as they please."

But presently the King went to the roaring hearth and, using black tongs, retrieved a pair of black iron slippers that had rested on the hot coals all day and night. He had made sure a constant supply of wood kept the fire going strong.

He placed the iron slippers before her, and nodded toward the open window, where yonder stood the black-hooded executioner with a large, silver iron ax resting upon his brawny shoulders.

But in stepped Snow White, as lovely a creature as ever lived, and as she stood before her stepmother, her countenance was grave and sorrowful. "I want you to know I forgive you for what you did to me, no matter what you say."

"Rubbish! I don't need your forgiveness, you stupid girl! I tried to kill you and I would do it again if I had the chance! I despise you!"

"But why? I never did any harm to you," Snow White answered, nearly weeping.

"You," the Queen said, her voice trembling with purple rage, "you represent everything I despise; you, with your stupid innocence and trusting nature, it is foolish girls like you who marry good but stupid men."

Snow White said, imploringly, "I want you to repent, to save yourself; if you do this, you will be banished from the kingdom, but you will live."

"Bah! I, a queen, repent? Repent for an act I would gladly do again?" she screamed, and she spied a sword hilt on a nearby soldier and lunged for it in an attempt to smite Snow White; but she was stopped, and thrown violently back toward the roaring hearth.

Snow White brought her hands in a supplicating gesture and knelt to the ground before her stepmother, weeping. "I beg you to repent sincerely of all your crimes so that you might avoid death."

The face of the Queen became eerily dark and savage as she spied the kneeling young woman, and as she was about to speak, her face blanched white in utter horror, for she now recognized the woman. "I know you, I know you from long ago; your name, your name is," and she pulled out her hair and stamped her feet, "your name is," and she thought of the name "Yxta" but she could not speak it, for it was forbidden here to speak of things that had not yet been. "You, I know you, and I know who I was, who I am, I was a queen then, and I am one now," and she stood erect and lifted up her face against them. "I will never bow before those of inferior rank."

And the King, full of remorse, instructed the soldiers to retrieve the red-glowing metal shoes out of the crackling fire and place them on the feet of the Queen, who proceeded to dance wildly about the small chamber. "Repent," whispered the citizens she had tormented and robbed, "repent and live," they shouted at her, "repent and feel sweet and innocent life for the first time."

But she would have none of it. "I curse all of you," she wailed in agony as she danced madly about her grim audience. "I am who I am, and I did what I did, and would do it again. You are treachery, and I am blameless! Curse you, curse you, curse you…" And presently her scorched and contorted body dropped to the ground, dead.

They buried her in a pauper's grave and soon she was forgotten, except by the birds of the air and the animals of the forest, who paid their respect to her the only way they could.

No good green grass ever grew over the small burial site of the vanquished Queen, but gnarled, tangled, weirdly-dressed-looking, blood-red weeds grew all over it and around it and atop it, and crooked and thorny weeds they were, which emitted a fetid smell that hovered over the mound like a seizing plague.

Back Again

Margaret was back again in Yxta's room, standing at Yxta's desk, in front of the children who sat solemnly at their desks. "Curse you two brats," Margaret finally said, after standing blank faced for several minutes, "I was a queen! No, I am a queen!"

Gretel looked at Margaret with a perplexity darkening her fair face. "Have you no shame at all? Did you not learn what you are? Do you not see that all of your actions are for your own gain, and that your hatred of all peoples is your greatest ambition?"

Margaret's wrinkled head turned to and fro, her face scrunched up in a bitter sneer, and her thin, purple lips mumbled nothing as she desperately sought an answer; but finally, she cried out, "You made me first a witch, then a queen of great power! Temptation! I am only human!" but she was speaking falsely now.

"But it does not matter," Hansel said, unmoved, "no matter the role you play, you are without moral merit or honor. You lastly had the power to do great and good things, and instead you used your power for wicked and vile acts."

"Lies, all lies," Margaret said, thinking all the while of a way out of her predicament.

"Do you repent of your cowardly sins?" Gretel asked, full of hope.

"Never!" Margaret returned, quickly, looking about the room, feigning to see something, "I have no sins to confess— cowardly—how dare you—and certainly none to you if I had any, you insufferable brats!" But she smiled then, full of guile, rubbing her swollen, purple-blotched hands together. "Well, why don't you two children release me and we'll forget the whole affair, and we can be fast friends; you would like that, wouldn't you? We'll have an ice cream together, wouldn't you like that, hmm?" she said, sickeningly sweet.

"Back you go," Hansel said, "and this time, the only command for you is that you must not harm innocent Snow White, and you will yet live."

"Nonsense! Snow White! And me, jealous of a little girl!"

"Prove that you do not despise all people and are not jealous of all pretty things, and you will live, old woman," Gretel said, her voice hard. "Now go."

One moment Margaret was standing in Yxta's room and slowly fading away with triumph smeared across her face just as if she had feasted greedily on its meaty pulp, and in the next moment she was back again, her body bedraggled, her face ravaged by calamity, her red-hot dance in the iron slippers once again having successfully shorn equanimity from her mind.

"Snow White must die," Margaret mumbled after several hours, still standing fast to the same spot in front of the wooden oak desk.

"She is who she is, there are no excuses," Gretel said to Hansel.

"Yes, she has no excuses before her."

"You aren't fair," Margaret finally whined. "You put me into situations doomed to failure, you want me to fail; it isn't my fault, you're against me, you want me to suffer. Give me a role of youthful innocence," she said, slyly, cocking her head to one side.

"Very well," Hansel said, "you wish to be someone innocent and free of the temptation of power; so, it will be as you
wish; and this time, you will remember all of this to the end."

"And this time," Gretel said, "there will be no excuses
if you fail; this time, you will have every chance to show
that you can be good; this time, you will be yourself from
youth, no bitterness or envy or strife from old age salting
your wounds."

One moment, Margaret was standing in the room
watching her two antagonists, and in the next, she was in a
small cottage, warming her strong, supple body in the warm
ashes of the brick hearth. She stood up and brushed off the
soot, and anxiously walked to the mirror to behold a young
woman of surpassing beauty. "I am young again, young and
pretty," Margaret exclaimed. It was true, so great was her
raw fleshly beauty that she seemed to be crafted from a sublime drawing made by a master artist; her eyes were an ebullient steel blue, and every line of her delicate face was drawn
in exact and deep hues of rosy red and scintillating white and
her lips were full and red and lush with the vital juices of
youth; her hair was thick and black and full and hung about
her strong, bare shoulders and above her comely small waist
and supple, slender legs. She stared in awe at this gushing
picture of consummate elegance and loveliness. She did not
recognize that the image she saw was from her own youth.

"Cinderella," a strident voice called out from the kitchen,
"get in here and serve us, you lazy wretch!"

"It's true, it's true," Margaret rejoiced within, "I am
young and beautiful, and innocent! I will show those two
brats who I really am!"

"Cinderella, you accursed wench, get in and make our
breakfast or I will hang you by your nails this very moment!"

Margaret slowly walked through the doors and beheld the collective brutality of her three mistresses. "Yes," she said to her stepmother.

Her stepmother frowned like a woman anxious for villainy. "Do you want a beating?"

Margaret, forging the idea of the story and her own life into one linear stream, knew her role to play. "No, Stepmother," she said, and eagerly fetched the morning meal for her stepmother and two stepsisters.

"Well, can you believe that little tart leaving the Prince again at the Grand Ball?" the stepmother said as she awaited her meal. "Why, the nerve of the little tease; does she think she will be his wife, especially when I have two very attractive daughters who are better suited for him?"

Margaret felt excitement spring up inside her and sweep over her tingling skin, and then she said, without guarding her thoughts, "Do you really think so, stepmother, with daughters who have such big feet…"

Her stepmother rose up with a hot biscuit in one hand and slapped Cinderella across her beauteous pink cheeks with her other. "You will speak when spoken to," she spat, "and speaking about your sisters in that fashion will bring you only grief," she finished, and sat down and continued eating.

Margaret stood up, red faced, thinking of revenge. But then a voice interrupted her dark reverie.

"Morning, my beautiful girls," a deep voice boomed into the kitchen. Margaret turned round and saw a big, robust-looking man, dressed in fine clothes and a big smile, walking through the back kitchen door. He hugged his stepdaughters and his wife, ignoring his own daughter.

"I don't remember you in this story," Margaret thought to herself. But she felt no loathing toward him, for he was not her father, and she had not yet acquired a hatred of all things men; for she was as she had never been, without a native loathing for any people and therefore wrapped in a gossamer cloak of innocence. She listened attentively as the family spoke of the ball that night, and how they planned on gaining access to the Prince for the daughters. Twilight descended upon the small cottage and the family departed for the palace, leaving Margaret to attend to her chores.

Margaret began to walk, as if drawn by a silence magnetic force, toward a small hill whereupon a large hazel tree grew; when she reached the grass-covered hill, she looked down and saw the grave of the woman who had birthed Cinderella, and as she lay upon it, she began to hear the delicate echoes of the past around her, as if those words spoken in truth and love still flitted and danced about the place; she heard a narration of a poor girl who lay in the warm ashes of the hearth every day to warm herself, and the cruel behavior of her stepsisters and stepmother toward her, and she listened intently how the stepmother and stepsisters readied themselves to attend the first night of the fete, and how Cinderella had begged to go, and how the stepmother had agreed only if Cinderella could pick a shovelful of lentils from the soot and ashes of the hearth; and how poor Cinderella had called upon the birds of the air to help her remove the lentils, and how she had then shown this to the stepmother, who had then declared that Cinderella could attend the ball if only she could retrieve two shovelfuls of lentils from the hearth, and how Cinderella again called upon the birds of the air to help her remove the lentils; but alas, the stepmother once again rebuffed her stepdaughter, and told her she could not go because she had no fine dress to wear; and how Cinderella had gone to the hazel tree and asked for a dress, and how the faithful birds had thrown down a dress of silver and gold, and how Cinderella had attended the ball and stolen the heart of the Prince but escaped from him when the affair was over and returned to her ashen bed, and how she had gone to the fete a second time in a dress, fairer still, and had once again enchanted the Prince, and once again eluded him as she ran back home. Margaret knew that she was surrounded by love and the protection of Nature and Heaven watching over her, and she then said, as if in a trance, "Shake and shiver, beautiful tree, throw gold and silver onto me." Then a bird appeared and threw down an elegant dress that sparkled with silver and gold, and a shining pair of small, golden slippers.

When she entered the ballroom at the palace, everyone was in amazement at her elegant beauty; even her stepmother and stepsisters did not recognize her. The Prince would dance only with her, and Margaret was pleased to receive such attention from such a wealthy man. But when it came time to leave, Margaret, despite her best intentions, felt a compulsion to go, and made various excuses to leave, and darted away.

But as this was the third time that Cinderella had come and enchanted the Prince and had eluded him after the fete the other two times, he was determined to find out who she was; so, beforehand he had prepared a stratagem to discover where his ladylove lived. He had ordered black pitch to be put on the steps of the castle, so when Cinderella hurried away, her left slipper became stuck in the black tar, and she was forced to leave it behind.

But it also must be told that many other guests too had their shoes stick to the black pitch, and some guests actually fell headlong down the stone steps and injured themselves;

and as a result of these occurrences there were many lawsuits and quarrels between the King and his royal guests. But that is a story for another time.

As it was, the lovelorn Prince sent for one of his servants and declared to him that no other should be his bride but the woman whose foot should fit into the gilded slipper.

Well, the messenger went from house to house with the shoe, but it appeared that no woman who had attended the ball had feet that fit; at last, the messenger went to the house of the two stepsisters. The eldest daughter and her mother went into another room to try on the shoe. "You would have a perfect fit if not for your big toe," the stepmother said and, grabbing a long, sharp knife out of the kitchen, she handed it to her eldest daughter. "Here, cut off that ugly growth; when you are a queen, you will not need your feet as much."

So, the elder sister cut off her big toe and painfully forced the shoe on and bravely stood up and appeared before the messenger, who then led her to the carriage and ordered the driver on toward the palace. But on the road they passed by the grave with the hazel tree, and two turtledoves sat upon the branches, crying,

"She is not the bride,
The shoe is too small,
Blood flows inside,
It does not fit at all."

Then the servant examined the shoe and found it soaked with blood, and so he ordered the coach turned round and allowed the next sister to try. So, she and her mother went into the next room, but her daughter could not get it over her bulging heel.

"Cut off some of that ugly hump," her mother said, handing her the same knife her sister had used. "As a queen, you will not be obliged to use your feet much." The mother fancied herself an expert on all things royal.

"Alack!" cried the youngest daughter, horrified. "How disgusting! Can we at least wipe the blood off it? What if there are weird things on that knife; I mean, what if, what if," and it seemed as if she was about to have an epiphany regarding the transmission of disease.

But her mother would have none of it, and she slapped this revolutionary idea right out of her daughter's head. "Now, stop your babbling and put on the shoe right now or I'll cut it all off myself!"

So, the maiden obeyed and cut off a significant piece of her heel, and then agonizingly stuffed the slipper over her foot and appeared before the messenger. But on the way to the palace, the coach had to go by the grave whereupon the hazel tree sat, and the two turtledoves cried once more:

"Back, go back
Blood is in the shoe
This shoe is way too small
This bride is false, and will not do."

So warned, the messenger examined the slipper and found it full of blood, and so ordered the sister back to her house; but then he went and retrieved the Prince and the both of them went to the house of Cinderella.

The Prince asked the father if he had any other daughters who might try on the gilded slipper, and the father said there was none, except a worthless daughter by his first marriage; but the Prince insisted on seeing this girl, and so the girl was sent for.

Margaret washed her face and hands and appeared before the Prince and tried on the shoe and it fit easily and the Prince knew it was she, his ladylove, and his heart soared with joy. He left the house full of women in a jealous rage.

As the royal coach passed by the hazel tree on the grave, the two turtledoves cried out,

"This is the maid, fair and true

Free of blood is her shoe,

This is the rightful bride inside,

And the rightful Prince at her side."

And as they drove on by, the two white doves flew into the coach and sat upon Cinderella's shoulders, one on the left and one on the right.

Margaret sat in a muted rage at the irksome birds who squatted atop her slender shoulders like they were wise sentinels; she ached to knock them off their sharp feet and out into the chilly air but she was restrained by what had to be and the role she had to play, for now; she was swept along by an enigmatic force where she walked between a force field of invisible walls and uttered words carved from a manuscript that would lead her to the proper destinations.

The day of the royal marriage came and the two stepsisters wished to weasel their way into the good fortune shared by Cinderella; and as the bridal party proceeded toward the church, each stepsister stood on either side of Cinderella. And as they walked, the two white doves swooped down and pecked out an eye from each of them. Now, people of even subnormal intelligence would have rushed to the hospital for help, but not these greedy sisters, no—they merely wrapped their injuries in white cloth and trembled in pain during the entire ceremony; and on the way back from the church, they changed places, one on the left and the other on the right of Cinderella, but once again the white doves flew down to them and picked out their remaining eye as easily as you or I might pick out a pit from a red cherry; and so, the stepsisters were blinded for their wickedness and falsehood the rest of their short and painful lives.

But this was not the end of them, no, indeed; they sought to live in peace with their mother, who soon drove them out, for as they were blind now and not apt to be married into any good fortune, they were no good to her. Thus, they became beggars on the muddy roads and perilous highways of the village, and eventually were robbed and beaten to death, their mangled corpses left to rot in the broiling sun.

As for the false stepmother, the queen of many wicked machinations, she plotted to murder her husband and gain his fortune for herself, but she failed in her attempt, and was sentenced to be hung; and as she suffered in prison, she conspired with two fellow inmates, by promising them vast riches to murder her traitorous husband; and shortly thereafter, she was led up to the wooden scaffold, where she was properly and slowly hung. And as for the husband, word was spread by the two fellow inmates that he had ample treasures buried about his cottage, and soon after his wife's death, robbers came for him in the middle of the night and tortured and eventually murdered him; alas, they found no treasure anywhere, and simply fled the dark place after setting fire to it.

Margaret came back from the wedding with her betrothed and sat down at a celebratory feast with her father-in-law, the King, and her mother-in-law, the Queen, and she listened to them speak affectionately of her and how they admired her Goodness and courage and steadfastness. The King took her aside and promised to be the kind of father her own father had not been, and the Queen took her aside and promised to be a good mother to her, and promised her she would always be there for her in any crisis, for she had no daughter, and would love her as her own child. On the walk home from the feast with the Prince, she heard the gentle doves and the birds of the air sing a song of rejuvenation to her, and the twinkling stars crowned her with a diamond crown fit for a princess, and the silvery moon christened her with silver beams of joy and wove a silver cloak of radiant joy around her, and when the morning came, and the Prince and Princess sat outside and watched the ruby-colored sky and pumpkin-colored sun raise its noble body above the far horizon, the warm shafts of sunshine bathed her in love and spoke rejuvenation to her, and the gentle breezes kissed her and rocked her and spoke love and rejuvenation and hope. The Prince bade her come in to the bedroom chamber, but she asked to stay awhile and enjoy the rosy dawn, and the birds of the air sang love and hope to her still, and the sunshine and the air and the morning dew spoke hope and innocence regained to her, and she heard it all, and listened to the inner workings of her heart, and then she scrunched up her beauteous face and said, "Bah! I don't trust any man," and she picked up a small rock and flung it at a nearby flock of white doves, and immediately she thought she heard a distant weeping, but she dismissed it and went into the bedroom chamber.

She stood before her husband, a lush, honey-scented vision of loveliness and vitality brimming with the raw lusts of youth in her long, snow-white gown; and yet she was still Margaret—Margaret as a precious girl of seventeen, her heart not yet turned to stone by the miseries of the world; and still, as she stood there and observed her man in his royal silken robes of lush gold, blue and white, she scrunched up her sour face and crossed her arms. "What are you after?" she grumbled. "Why are you with me, when you could have any woman in the kingdom?" He once more declared his undying love for her and his deep adoration for her and once again promised to be faithful and true to her all his days, but she was not moved. "It's just lust, you fool; you don't know what love is!" she nearly screamed. "And I won't let you have your brutish way with me."

But he remonstrated in earnest, and then said, "You married me, Cinderella; you vowed to be faithful to me and stay with me."

Margaret giggled, hands on hips now. "Well, I admit that I liked all that attention and finery, what girl wouldn't? But what about after the wedding, what do I do then, eh?"

"You will have your wifely duties, of course," he replied, thinking he was pacifying her, and proceeded to describe what she was to do while he was away battling dragons and fighting in wars and visiting foreign lands.

"What! Walk around in royal clothes all day and smile and wave? I would rather go back to the stone hearth and lie in the ashy soot."

They argued all that dark day and all that black night and into the next violet dawn, until the Prince finally fled and took refuge in his father's castle, leaving Margaret very smug and happy to have driven out her husband. "He is cunning," she said, walking outside in the royal gardens in her sienna-colored dress, and she heard the bluebirds and the white doves sing to her and the golden sunshine hum to her and the fragrant air whistle a tune to her, all of whom were serenading her with the same song of hope and love and rejuvenation, and she cocked her head and listened and frowned and picked up a rock and flung it toward the birds. "Leave me alone, you troublesome brats! Go and mind your own business!"

The Prince found that if he proffered his wife precious gifts, she would join him in the bedroom chamber, and in due time, she became extremely wealthy, gaining much praise from the aristocracy for her business acumen; but this arrangement with her husband lasted only until Margaret had all the necessary funds with which to sustain herself and declare herself independent of her husband.

In a few years she had amassed a great fortune by bickering and bartering and trading with diverse kingdoms and merchants and peoples of all persuasions, often cheating them and swindling them and blackmailing them while she hid behind the golden armor of her husband's army; and the King tried to dissuade her and the Queen begged her to relent but this Margaret would not do, for she felt the engine of power stirring in her, and she would not be cowed to appease her family, nor humbled to appease her kingdom.

She had her own adjutants and her own royal court and her own personal army that surrounded her like a vast moat. She hired archers to shoot all birds within a mile radius of her newly built palace, and she erected great stone walls and a giant black dome to keep out the sunshine; she kept inside this insular stronghold as she plotted her schemes against the increasing amount of people in the kingdom who seemed to be her enemies. She entered into secret trysts with foreign kingdoms, promising them great riches if they helped her to topple the King and Queen.

She had long ago drowned the two males born to her by the Prince, by putting the newborns in a dirty, brown knapsack and then tying the ends with rope and gleefully tossing the wiggling and crying infants into the icy-cold river. And the sunshine wept over her and begged her to repent, and the birds of the air sang a chorus of repentance for her, and the wind strummed a tune of humility and forgiveness to follow, but she raised her fist at all of them and cursed the precious Light they brought, and returned to her domed and dank dungeon.

But she saw the necessity of securing vast riches for her grandiose plans, and as she still retained some of her innate beauty, she beguiled a wealthy duke to join her in her attack on the King and Queen; so, she lay with him and within a year she had secretly borne him a male child.

Now, she could not hide all of her wicked plans from her husband, for he had long since placed spies within his wife's organization. It was a cold, gray, blustery day when he enticed her to dine with him and his parents in the royal castle, and she reluctantly agreed, arriving in her now-customary long, black dress and black leather shoes, her milk-white complexion evincing calm and surpassing certitude.

The royal family ate in silence most of the meal, until the Prince stood up and declared that he would do all he could to win back the trust and love of his beloved wife, but Margaret scoffed at this and said she would rather die than live with him again in a subservient role. His face became somber. "Then, you have chosen."

"I chose nothing," she grunted, eating her meat pie. "You brought me here as a prize, but I am my own woman, and I do my own will."

"Even if that will is treason," the Prince said, slyly, watching his wife drop her fork. "Yes, my lovely wife, treason of the highest order, treason against my father and my mother; treason against me I can forgive, but what you have done is unforgivable; and yet, I still forgive you, despite the murder attempts on my parents; yes, I know about that, too, and the secret treaties and the promises to other rulers. Do you deny any of it?"

Margaret stood up, her face purple with rage. "I deny none of it! You are weak," she shouted, waving at them. "This kingdom needs a strong hand," and she pounded her chest, "me! I will rule! My hand will make this country strong and feared!"

"But there are no wars, now, they have been forgotten; you are attempting to start wars simply to gain what you do not need; you already have power and wealth and family; Cinderella, why, why do you do these horrible things? What happened to the brave and noble girl I married?"

Margaret scowled as she walked around the room, pausing behind the King and Queen, both of whom sat in the bosom of melancholy. "This is who I am, me; this is who I am no matter where I go or what I do," and she remembered who she really was and why she was here—she had always the ability to remember this time—but she had dismissed it. "I am who I am, I need power over the lives of others; and I will have it," she cried in a terrifying voice, and then she sat down and began to eat once more the exceptionally chunky, pungent pie.

The Prince hung his head low. "Then, you have condemned yourself."

"And what will you do?" she said, arrogantly. "Have me arrested?"

The King, who had said nothing the entire time, looked with regret at his daughter-in-law, and then spoke, his voice full of pathos and sorrow, "I loved you like a daughter, and would have done anything for you, and this is how you repay me; why, why," he let his head fall into his hands, "why are you thus?"

Margaret laughed, throwing back her head so that her long, ebony hair fell off her shoulders. "You, who are so weak, how can you know someone who is so strong? You haven't the courage to even punish your own."

The King grew solemn. "Oh, but you are wrong, Cinderella, so very wrong, indeed," he said, eerily, and he held up his head on high, and looked to the food she was gobbling as if she were a common peasant. "Are you enjoying your meal?"

"Well," she replied, lips pursed, "it is rather tough and salty, but it will do."

The King let his head fall to one side as he gazed at her. "Then, you will appreciate what is inside the pie."

Margaret abruptly dropped her fork and retched.

"That is right, my daughter, whom I loved like my own child; you think me weak, but that is a mistake on your part; you see, in times of peace, there is no reason to show strength or cruelty; but in times of trouble, as now; yes," his voice grew grave, "the meal you eat is the flesh of your flesh, the son you bore in your adulterous affair with your lover, who now lies in the swamp with a dozen arrows piercing his traitorous body." He watched, equanimity flowing throughout his royal veins, as Cinderella stood up and vomited her meal onto the finely polished floor. "You have caused great distress in our kingdom," he said, "and many have died to undo what you did; your wicked heart has sealed your fate," and he motioned to his guards, who stood outside in the hallway, to seize her.

At her trial, Margaret was given the chance to repent for her crimes against the state. "Bah!" she cried. "Me, repent, for what, for being strong and ambitious?" She shook her fist at the royal family. "All of you seek to repress women and keep power in the hands of men," and she pounded her chest, "but this woman would not let it be so! I know what I did and I am proud of it and would not undo any of it! I am me, I am like the wolf who hunts the rabbit and the squirrel; I must obey my nature!" She howled and barked and tore at her heavy black chains as the royal family looked on in amazement. She cursed them and reviled them and spat at them. "I need to feel power, power, power flowing through me," she cried, and her hands joined together as she raised them up toward the vaulted ceiling, and her voice became eerily low, as if she were whispering to powerful forces unseen, and her countenance grew dark and wild, as if an invisible force had taken possession of her, "I must rule over those around me, for I am superior to all—all are peasants, and I am a queen, a queen, a queen..." And as she fell to the cold floor, callous maledictions spilled out of her mouth like a scavenging black oil that bubbled and boiled and searched for innocents to devour; but when its execrable nature touched the hem of the royal family, it rose up in screeching agony and fled back into the gaping mouth of its master, a sanguinary, dagger-filled mouth like that of the howling, black wolf.

As Margaret was led to the wooden scaffold, the pious birds of the air sang repentance to her and the warm sunshine whispered love and hope and rejuvenation and the perfumed breezes implored her to forgive and forget, but she cursed them and spat at them. She was led up the brown wooden steps and onto the crimson platform whereupon resided the big man with the bulging muscles and black hood and large steel ax that sat upon his brawny shoulders. A priest was there to offer solace but she plowed her round head into his soft belly and knocked him to the waiting crowds below. She stood before the people and laughed and mocked them, and they shrank away in terror at the withered mask she now wore and the unearthly glow that emanated from her grim face. The King, staring from his palace window, once more begged Cinderella to repent and save her own life, but he found only scorn and cursing from her in return; thus relieved of all guilt, he issued the final order; and then Margaret was forced to her knees and her head placed on the hard, cold stump of the tree so that it hung over the bloodstained edge; and then the executioner lifted the weighty ax and as it came down, it cleft the air and a fervent song whistled out which begged that Margaret repent of her crimes; and yea, Margaret seemed to hesitate for a moment as she considered the offer, but expelled a loud curse and scrunched up her face and felt the cold steel penetrate her neck, and then her head was separated from her body as it fell into the brown straw basket below.

The crowd did not cheer, but merely turned round and walked back home, sorrowful that their heroine had died so ignobly. And as for Margaret, her body was buried separately from her head, in two deep holes, many acres apart, in a place that the Prince soon had submerged in water and that later became a swamp no earthly creature dared to visit.

The kingdom was covered in a kind of heavy, thick ash for a very long time until a low whisper began to go forth that spoke of rewards to the faithful and new beginnings and the promise of the story beginning all over again, and before long, all tears were wiped away and bad memories forgotten and there was a young prince who needed a wife and he was giving a royal ball at the palace.

Everyone went home again.

Freedom

Hansel and Gretel stood, solemnly.

Hansel spoke, his tone one of judgment. "You have proven who you are, and so you will be. You are who you are, as you have rightly said. But now the Third Level awaits you."

"Repent, ye sinner, or die in thy sins," Gretel said, sorrowfully. "One soul lost to the lusts and promises of sin is a tragedy."

"You and your ridiculous stories," Margaret shouted, after waking up from her heavy lethargy, and looking about the room she was in once more, "you send me to places that aren't real," and she waved it all away with a vicious snarl, and began to remember her life there, and she mumbled, smiling, as she placed her fisted hands underneath her sagging chin. "I had so much fun, though…"

But then Margaret felt a weight lifted from her, and her left foot rose up, and as she looked toward the two children, she saw that they were gone; and therefore, to celebrate their departure, she danced a wild jig around the room.

She was not foolish enough to think the whole affair with the two children just a dream, but neither did she care about their boasting of the Third Level; for, truth be told, there was no alteration in her character she thought she could make to appease them. "I am not bad, or worse than everybody else," she mumbled as she carefully moved about the room, spying into every corner, speaking clearly and carefully just in case her two tormentors were still listening. "And I don't know what to change—oh, bah! I'm as good as any person." When she realized that the children were indeed gone, her former character completely returned. "Why, I'm better than most people! Ha! Try and cause me to change; why," her eyes widened, "I'll bet it was all a test to see if I could be tempted to do evil; maybe," she rubbed her sagging chin, "Level Three is Heaven—heh, heh!"

She walked around the school that night feeling superior to all living things, and she became emboldened in her grand design to discover all those things her employees did. Standing in the pod area, which was adjoined to the classrooms, she realized that these small areas had no cameras. "We shall see about that," she bellowed, and after studying the state guidelines regarding the surveillance systems, she became disheartened. "No cameras allowed in lounges or pod areas—bah!" Thus determined to thwart the rules, she set up an aluminum ladder next to the main office building and ascended its metal rungs.

"Well, any place we drill a spy hole must be inconspicuous," she murmured to herself and, walking to the edge, looked over the black-tarred roof.

There was a small, plastic, black flying disk that sat, unbeknownst to her, next to her feet, thrown up to the roof by a naughty student. In days past, custodians would have noticed the toy and all other such objects during their weekly sweeps atop the roof, but since recesses were banned, this practice of the custodians had been discontinued.

When Margaret turned from the ledge, the plastic soles of her red shoes met the plastic sole of the round disk, and the result rendered a slight wobble in her slumped form. Looking down, she saw the disk and cursed it, and meant to kick it, but missed, and her poor balance sent her teetering precariously close to the edge of the roof, where, for a few seconds, she appeared like a marionette, dancing slowly with those teasing puppet masters, Hope and Despair. Then, she lost her breath, for she was in midair.

The flight did not last long—from takeoff to destination was a mere heartbeat in length—but the landing was memorable for her as she struck a great, gnarled oak tree, and she was quickly caught among its thick, sturdy branches.

Outrage tickled her for a moment, and she began to curse this situation, but she soon realized no sound escaped from her lips. A spindly, singular round loop of tree branch had secured itself around her scrawny neck, and she was slowly gasping for air, her own weight pulling her down while it was pulling up on this Nature's noose.

Everything she loathed she thought of, everything she despised about the world scurried across the dying pastures of her mind, and she blamed the entire world for her dilemma.

"Is it a dream again," she cried in her private horrors. "Have those two brats sent me here?" Nay, but this was no dream, and the air, unable to get to her mouth or nostrils, decided to go elsewhere with its precious cargo and pleasure an appreciative organism.

Margaret soon expired, and she dangled like a victim of a mob lynching from inside the woody home of the accommodating tree.

Alas, all of her body did not die, even though decay began to set in. A mortal death had indeed occurred, but a deeper layer of life, like an underground stream, preserved her senses.

During the night she thought she was alive, just as any person might conclude, and when rosy-colored dawn came and scrubbed away the inky blackness of the night, and the unseasonably warm sun swaddled her in its golden beams, the natural processes of decay came to fruition.

She was hanging from a tall, stout tree that was situated between two buildings in the back of the school, in a place surrounded by natural barriers of other buildings and trees. No casual passerby could see her.

"If only those brats who play ball on the field would come by," she raged, as she still felt the agony of her neck being stretched. But the children no longer came; perhaps they might have been there even the night it happened, but Margaret had succeeded in chasing them away days before by calling the local authorities and lodging an official complaint against the children.

"But I'm still alive," she boasted to herself, not knowing that the natural death known to all people had already occurred.

By twelve o'clock noon, the sun was baking her, and her decaying flesh began to put out a putrid odor that wafted into her preserved senses. "Egad!" she cried in utter disgust. "What a stench! Where is everybody? Help me!" Her mind lapsed into babbling and rambling, and then would peep out on occasion to see if rescuers had come. Her physical torment increased.

Insects are foraging creatures, living to reproduce, gather food and eat. In their wandering, they will cover every inch of terra firma with their incessantly moving antennae and feet. Let them find a great quantity of food, and in an hour's time, these decomposers will have enveloped the entire plant or animal with their industrious colony.

So, it was no surprise to find that when a large black ant that was crawling up the tough limbs of the oak bumped into Margaret's rotting corpse, it bit off a sliver of her savory flesh and then scurried back to its hole. In a short while, the hungry scavengers were excitedly crawling all over the hanging dead body.

"Eh, what's this?" Margaret yelled in her feverish mind. "Egad! Ants are crawling all over me! Help!" It was the last ejaculation of unrefined fright that echoed like the roar of a trapped lion in a cage, and for hours this loud wail of hers was all she communicated to her dissipating sanity.

Now, to exacerbate her dilemma, her small eyes were stuck wide open, so that she might see all that befell her, and on top of this, her gray eyes had already bulged out and given her a more cinematic view of her position.

Ants were only the prelude to the feast that was embarking eight feet up the mighty oak tree, for diverse kinds of creatures came to gain their daily nourishment, and some of them were, but not limited to: crickets, spiders, worms, grasshoppers, flies, brown sparrows, and even an occasional raven. The munching and crunching and crawling and excruciating noise of the feeders seeded Margaret's collapsing mind with more incoherent rambling that sprouted and spread like wildfire until she simply screamed and hollered in torment during every waking moment.

It was impossible for her to lose consciousness, and into every creature's mouth went her sentient mind.

Maggots were laid in her putrefying flesh, and the squirming youngsters soon hatched. Her eyeballs, with yellow worms coming out of them, fell out, and as they dropped to the ground, she could still see through them; and presently a large, gaping mouth opened up and swallowed both of them. "Arf," barked the dog, begging for more tasty nuggets.

Margaret had accidentally left a side gate open that morning and a pack of stray dogs had trotted through it, and these same dogs were now thirsty and possessing a voracious appetite. It was when the dogs began to pull on her rotting legs with their sharp teeth, and then began to chew and gulp her, that she went convincingly, unavoidably, and perfectly mad.

The dogs certainly gobbled up her fragmented corpse despite the lack of muscle upon its miserly form, eventually pulling her down and chomping into her just as if she were a savory bowl of dog chow.

The birds of the field helped to pick her bones clean, while the insects gobbled every tiny scrap of edible tissue the large creatures missed; in less than three days' time, all that was left of her were her blanched, white porous bones strewn about her red dress with the white polka dots, and other equally dirty garments.

Not a single person had missed her, as she was not one to socialize or even be at her house longer than an overnight stay, just as if her home were a hotel; thus, no one knew she was gone, not even her son Roger, who had escaped a year earlier from his mother's iron grip by marrying a strong woman and eloping with her to a distant land, thus embittering Margaret even more against men; and so her gruesome remains were finally discovered by the custodians upon their return to work after the New Year. Her identity was soon confirmed through dental records.

The interim Principal, a middle-aged woman with a stolid countenance, made the official announcement to the staff at a meeting after school during their first week back. "Well, I have sad news," she began, and at that crucial moment, the staid faces of the Teachers changed to one of frothy anticipation, for they had just then brought themselves back from their special places. "It seems apparent that Mrs. Carbuncle died here during the holiday session in a freak…"

Ah, but the Teachers no longer heard the mindless ramblings of yet another common administrator; in its stead, they heard the wild celebrations of victory inside their merry minds.

"What are the chances she faked her own death," James asked, in earnest, about to burst, "just to catch us off our guard?"

"How dare you!" the administrator exclaimed and, looking about, noticed that no tears had been shed, no face was veiled in sorrow, except, of course, the MSs'.

Then, one of the female Teachers, who had nearly been driven to a mental breakdown by Mrs. Carbuncle's relentless persecutions, began to weep, and presently, all could see that her crying was merely a misinterpreted prelude, for they saw that the silver pearls trickling down her face were of a pristine joy, and she began to laugh so loud and so hard and so unabashed that immediately the other Teachers, those who were not aligned to the vanquished enemy, laughed with her, as if all of them had just been released from the dungeons after serving a long, torturous sentence for a crime they had not committed. All kinds of hilarity erupted.

Women were lifting up their skirts to their knees and dancing like can-can girls on tabletops.

The celebration poured outside to the fresh, delicious Winter air, where grown men danced wildly about with their index fingers atop their head, and they twirled and skipped about like they were children in a giddy fit.

James ran to his room and brought back a special song that would magnify and illuminate the mood of his colleagues; he plopped it into the tape recorder and then placed it next to the speakerphone of the public announcement system. In a second, a chorus of deep-throated male baritones was singing about the death of a certain wicked witch.

O, the gaiety this song caused throughout the campus as the Teachers joined in to recite the endearing lyrics; some Teachers twirled arm in arm while they danced like revelers at a victory festival, and others merely laughed or turned cartwheels or performed any other childish act they felt compelled to do.

The temporary Principal sat motionless in her office, not wanting to get involved in the chaos.

When the mass catharsis was nearly over for the Teachers, the MSs, acting as a single organism, moved out from the office and into the cement courtyard to confront the joyous Teachers.

"You have no right to desecrate Mrs. Carbuncle's good memory," one of Carbuncle's most fervent, and now tearful, patriots screamed at them.

"Good?" Yxta shouted back, unafraid, her smile fading slowly. "What was good about that old witch? She brought nothing but destruction to our school!" Everyone abated their festivities, and stood fast, anger now cradling their thoughts. "Margaret Carbuncle was a plague upon this place," she continued, her comely face lit by righteous indignation; "she hurt the children, destroyed a fine family of Teachers, mocked the idea of a quality education; why, I celebrate her death." She was about to cry, but her pride and honor held her composure together. Her tone was a guttural shout now, trembling with rage as she walked up, fully erect, to her accusers. "And I hope, no, I pray to God in Heaven that this school gets a great principal who not only wipes out your precious Queen's sick legacy, but takes care of her loyal crew." She sneered violently. "You sicken me." She held up her head high as she whispered with all the passionate glory in her shining heart to these shocked women. "I can hear all of you now," she said in a fierce guttural tone, "'I was just following orders,'" and she spat at their feet.

"Go, girl," James whispered, his eyes twinkling with admiration.

As it turned out, the new Principal was merely another disciple of the Superintendent, thus confirming the old proverb that "a rotten tree puts forth no good fruit." Sadly, the Teachers soon resumed their comfortable stay in their private Utopias.

However, as if to confirm yet another old adage, "corrupt things inevitably fall under their own corrupt weight," the Superintendent and his ruthless gang of assistants were, within the year, indicted for fraud and theft and graft involving district money.

A new Superintendent came in like the noble sheriff of old who cleans up the lawless town. Every one of the accomplices of the old Superintendent and his loyal subordinates at the District Office fell from grace, and concurrently, a shout of triumph spilled from the joyous lips of the Teachers.

And then the state rescinded the order to have cameras installed in the classrooms.

"Paradise no more," James said one fine Autumn day to Yxta as he pointed to his head, and then, pointing to the school, "Paradise here."

A year later, Yxta gave birth to a beautiful baby girl. James married Celeste a week later.

The Fate of Saffron

And what became of Saffron, after the tide of Power she had ridden was evaporated? Her time within the district was gone, for she had thrown her lot into the wrong corner and now she had to move on. She applied to many districts, but none would have her now, for the story of her immediate Mistress and her ignominious downfall and the subsequent scandals associated with her and her superiors crawled all over Saffron like slimy worms in every desperate interview she gave; she had been blacklisted just as she had blacklisted others, she was an outcast just as she had outcast others; but she had thrown Innocents into a gentle stream where they had washed ashore onto Paradise, while she was thrown into a swirling storm and dragged down into the tempestuous sea.

She even lowered herself into the humble station of teaching, and one district even hired her, but she could not suffer the orders given to her from her masters, and so she soon quit and lost her teaching credential as a result. Her marriage dissolved. She moved into a small apartment and found solace in various prescription pills and hard liquor. She did not leave her tiny abode for days, drugged out and drunk and sprawled on the floor in her own waste; and even in her misery, she begged for mercy and repented of her sins; but no help came for her, only the throbbing torment of physical agony and mental anguish, and she thought she would go mad and hoped herself insane, wished herself dead, not only for her ignoble existence but for her past crimes against those whom she once embraced. But still, no hope came, and she languished as if one dead, a sickly recluse, a hollowed-out, battered and beaten woman who was flailed by the past and tormented by the present; she could not move this way or that without remembrance of what she had been before she was seduced by the dark side of Power, a power like an infection that she now saw as insignificant and absurd. "Real Power is in love and compassion," she would now say, staring at the empty bottles of liquor strewn about her dirty place. "I was weak when I thought I was strong, and now I have lost all, because I could not see beyond the moment," she murmured, and she would weep at such times, even for days on end. And as she wept and repented, she reasoned she would be rescued by someone or something, somehow, some way, because now she was different and only wanted to show the world she could be as she once was.

Month after month came and her physical body deteriorated and her mental health waned and then she wished more often for death. She often lamented that death was the only way out for her, and so on one cold, dark and rainy day she bought many bottles of sleeping pills and copious bottles of alcohol and planned to consume them all at once to finally end this funeral march that had dragged on much too long. She decided on a particular dreary, foggy night and she had all the bottles in front of her and she stared at them for hours as does the man who stares at the blank walls in his prison cell as he waits for the executioner. She would reach for the pills and pull her shaking hand back and then reach again for the liquor and pull her trembling hand back, each time sobbing and trembling, knowing that these would be her last moments on Earth; and still, she secretly hoped for rescue, and she prayed to God and she prayed and prayed and hoped and wept and lay on her silver sofa and stared up at the vague ceiling and wondered how any of it had occurred; and then she screwed up her courage and abruptly sat up and grabbed the first white bottle of pills and opened the plastic cap and raised it her dry lips.

A knock came at the door.

The pills spilled all over the floor and the sofa as Saffron jumped out of her skin. She did not know what to think or what to do but she stood up and walked over to the door and opened it and nearly fainted when she saw who stood before her.

"Hello, Saffron," Yxta said, smiling.

Saffron did not know what to do, but she smiled in return and stood there, embarrassed now that she and her apartment were in the tattered state they were in, and she had the presence of mind to move closer to Yxta to prevent her from peering inside the spoiled place. "Yes," she said, her mind in a fog, and then she was vexed that her former friend would come here, and her voice was ghastly, like the poisonous fumes that leak out of a condemned house, "and what do you want?"

Yxta, accustomed to all kinds of behaviors, was unmoved. "I came here to help."

There, the words Saffron had prayed for and begged for were proclaimed, and now Hope stood before her, but she was not pleased, for she had reasoned her old friends would come for her, her old acquaintances from school, the MSs, but who should stand before her now but an old foe?

Yxta smiled, as only a woman can in such situations, and commenced to explain it all. "It was James' idea, and Joy thought it grand, too, and so all of us decided to find out about those who had followed her and had fallen out of favor in society; and James found some, and Joy found some, and others found some more, but only a few of them wanted help and some did not need help, and some had even died." She watched as a portent of doom passed over the face of her listener. "We offered help because we knew it was the right thing to do, even though we knew we didn't have to do it; well, it's hard, you know." Her voice became melancholy. "You are persecuted and then you are free, and it is hard to forgive your tormentors, and many do that, but it is even harder to try and help them get back to the Light; but I guess that is the way of things and the way it should be, to want people to do good and be on the right side; I know I am sounding righteous and blunt but that is the way it is and I see no other way to say it, and now I will say it again: I am here to help you," and she just stopped, just like that, staring with a loving and gentle face at someone who had once been her taskmaster.

Saffron just stood there, numb and confused and wondering what to do, thinking of the past and present and looking at and through Yxta and beyond to her own impending dark grave and her loneliness and the abject squalor that surrounded her, and then she just fell to her knees and wept like a newborn baby. Yxta picked her up and took her inside and helped her to the sofa and presently they talked and talked and talked and then cleaned the apartment as they talked and talked and talked some more.

A month later, Saffron applied to regain her teaching credential, and with the guidance of her new friends, she received it, and two months hence, she was sitting in a room waiting to be interviewed for a teaching position. There were three letters of recommendation in her portfolio, recommendations from people she had once known and then knew again, and she smiled as the man called her name and she went into the small office; but she was not alone as she walked in, because Hope and Friendship and Love walked in with her, and she was not afraid.

Judgment Day

Every creature that had eaten a piece of Margaret carried her sentient consciousness in them, and through them she felt a remarkable scope of pain bludgeoning her mind.

She felt their razor-sharp teeth rip into her skin and suck her mottled blood, heard their tearing and chewing of her muscle into bits. She experienced the excruciating agony of their digestive juices as they dissolved her remains into a formless blob, and then she felt herself excreted out of the creatures onto the land.

Her consciousness, still imbedded into her sinewy remains, trickled down into a porous soil that filtered all kinds of debris, and when she had reached the deep river of cool water that flowed under the ground, her bodily remains had been purified, and she became a few specks of organic matter.

Her widely scattered bits of self united into a single clump of matter as it bubbled along in the underground water table, and Margaret had no thoughts as she experienced exotic wonders no human being could ever experience.

During this magical sojourn through the Earth's outer crust, Margaret, seeing and feeling and hearing all, appreciated none of it. Where there were thick veins of sparkling gold, clusters of prismatic crystals of pink and blue, and rich deposits of translucent, sparkling gems, she saw only colored dirt; where there were ancient ruins of long-forgotten civilizations, she saw rotting wood and broken chunks of clay; and where there was a vast cavern of ebullient water coursing toward the ocean, she heard only irritating noise. She cursed it all, every natural wonder and man-made structure, for she yearned only to be queen again of her private castle.

Spilling out into the majestic ocean, Margaret's essence floated along in the gentle currents among the teeming marine life, and she cursed them. She despised the intrinsic beauty of the cluster of white coral and the deep blue pitch of water, and the multicolored fish and the swaying green plant life about her. In it all, she saw only chaos and ugliness, and she questioned the natural order of things.

Her pain had long since vanished, and her mind rested without physical disturbance, sitting in a tranquil, wistful suspended state, able not only to penetrate the great wonders around it, but to absorb its unique, individual signature. All of it meant nothing to her because she had no use for it.

Drifting in the warm, swirling currents of the sunlit sea for a time that spanned many seasons, Margaret felt herself being pulled upward through the ethereal air to rest in the soft, argent puffs of clouds.

"This is life," whispered the sunbeams; "life is joy and beauty."

"Enjoy the serenity of nature," spoke the wind.

"Feel the gentle soul of the universe," sang the clouds.

But Margaret scoffed at it all.

The great expanse of cerulean sky opened itself to her as the cumulus congestus clouds swam in the warm streams of air; it hovered above radiant hills and pristine lakes; it breezed past majestic mountains and fields and pastures of tall, green grasses and brightly colored, scented flowers.

This cumulus cloud would dissipate and Margaret's essence would accumulate in another cumulus variety, and her mystical journey would continue across the continents. She saw life in its naked form, all living creatures, good and bad, great and small, traveling hither and thither. She saw their joys and hopes and loves and sorrow; yet, she saw nothing that resembled her life, her dreams and hopes and desires, so she dismissed all of it as degrading sentimentality and weakness of mind. She condemned the good times of the people as moments of laziness.

One day she felt herself descending from the cloud and falling to the Earth in the form of a raindrop, but she never made it to the soil, for she fell, instead, onto a woman's bare head, where she was absorbed into the woman's bloodstream, and fell into the woman's cells and into her very DNA; but she found it incompatible, and then moved on to the woman's mind, where she experienced the woman's Goodness, but she rejected it and was ultimately deposited in the woman's rich, jade-colored eyes.

In the woman's home, Margaret saw the love and joy of family life; she saw the man and woman with their many children, and she saw them celebrate the blessings of good health and sharing and kindness. She saw their unbound Love for each other, and Margaret despised it all, for she had reasoned long ago that Love did not exist but was an artificial bond that kept a woman enslaved to a man.

At the woman's work, Margaret soon realized the woman was a Teacher who taught elementary school children, and she heard dialogue in the classroom that confused and frightened her.

"Mrs. Beryl," one of the female students asked, "tell us again when they used to have video cameras in here. Were you nervous?"

Yxta smiled and her green eyes glistened. Margaret hated it when these orbs she was in glowed with Moral Virtue.

"Well, sometimes," Yxta smiled, "but Teachers fought for their rights, just as other groups we have talked about fought for their rights."

"The Bill of Rights," one of the girls exclaimed.

"Exactly," Yxta said, proudly.

"Why didn't everyone just quit?" asked one of the bright male students. "And there was that mean old woman, Mrs. Carbuncle, who was worse than any rude surveillance camera."

All of the students moaned at the mention of Mrs. Carbuncle's name.

Now, Yxta was remembering the way it was, and how everyone thought it would never change. "Sometimes," she murmured, "you just have to stand and fight," and she smiled when she thought of her special place, which she sometimes went to no matter where she was, "even if it is in a way people do not understand. I suppose it is the idea of the last person standing…"

At lunch, Yxta was in the bathroom, looking into the mirror, remembering what her family had said to her when the persecution from Margaret had been at its zenith. "Why do you stay, Yxta? You know what this woman did to you! You lost your baby, Yxta! I know they have made it difficult for you to find a position elsewhere, but you must go!"

Yxta stared at her beauteous face in the mirror, looking intently into teary eyes. "Injustice," she whispered with great emotion to herself; "I stayed to fight; let the weak go; this is my school, my district, my students, my family," and she allowed her pious tears to flow in steady channels down her florid cheeks.

Her warm tears fell silently into the white sink and were flushed down into its piping and into the sewer system.

"Why was I with that weak woman?" Margaret wondered as she now beheld sewage floating about her. "I never cried a day in my life! And how dare those children talk about me like that! I was a queen!"

The journey in the sewer canals was brief, and soon Margaret landed in a steel holding tank at the water district treatment plant. In a moment, she merged with a microorganism that ate sludge.

"Egad, what a horrible stench!" she cried, her senses restored again. "I am so very hungry, but to eat this filth all day. Ugh!" But she was a Rotifer Philodina now, living on the discards of people and their waste, helping to clean the sewage water so that later it could be deposited on land again.

The seasons passed, and Margaret ate her own weight in excrement a million times over, quite often the very same waste of those whom she had persecuted.

Margaret ate for eight hours daily, and then rested for a sufficient time, and then ate again; if, perhaps, sludge wasn't available to her, then her instinct led her to eat other protozoa and metazoa.

She lusted for the most virulent, raunchy-tasting human waste, all the while cursing everyone and everything.

And then a cycle began where she was eaten by bigger microorganisms, and she felt the horror and pain of being devoured; but then she would be excreted out of them and be absorbed by lesser organisms, and became sentient in their bodies, until, once more, they were eaten by a large microorganism, but then she would be freed from them and once again she would be whole and eager to devour all in her way as she gained great strength and stature.

"This is who you are," sang a chorus of other sludge-eating microorganisms, "this is your life! Queen of the excrement-eating creatures—think, think, why you are here!"

Margaret scorned all of this talk, and soon she developed a great desire for the sludge, and she began to order the other microorganisms about as is if she indeed were their queen.

"I am not beaten, merely bruised," Margaret thought to herself, watching the other parasites cower before her. "This is my destiny! I am a natural-born leader!"

But one day she was flushed from her kingdom of sewage, and once more she fell to the ground and was purified through the natural filters of the soil, where she entered the water table, spilled out into the ocean, and immediately rose up into the serene sky.

This time she flew to the great vaults of Heaven, wherein she beheld an effulgent, white light, and she trembled before it.

"Art Thou God?" Margaret whispered. "Must I ask Thee for an invitation into Thy kingdom?" She frowned, for questions streamed into her mind. "What have I done for Thee? Well," she mused for a while, "I haven't killed anybody." She stood, aghast at her own admission of guilt. "Why did I treat Thy children with such cruelty? Well, they are inferior! What? My heart is wicked and filled with hatred against Thy Holy Creation?" She began to become indignant, and held her head up high, but her words were silenced, and then in a little while, she continued. "Eh? I was shown the error of my ways by those two little brats? And I never appreciated the sublime gifts of Nature after I died and traveled about? Bah! I can't see what I can't see! Thou tortured me! How is that supposed to make me into a better person?" She was silent again. "I have rejected Love and Justice and Kindness all my life and replaced them with enmity and scorn and injustice for my fellow Man and Nature itself? Well, Thou are entitled to Thy opinion." She sneered. "And Thou sayest I rejected Thee? Ha! Now I have Thee! When did that happen? Thou were in every act of kindness that I rejected, in every breath of Nature's beauty I scorned, in every precious moment of Love I refused? I never saw that. And Yxta," she scrunched up her face, "she spoke of Thee, yes, but how was I to know? This isn't fair. Say," she smiled, staring coyly at the great expanse of translucent white light, "just reincarnate me or something—no? Well, how about if I just run up Thy sleeve—I read that in a book once—I just run up Thy sleeve and Thou, a forgiving God, send me back so I can get it right. You will do this because Thou are a benevolent God and we aren't really responsible for our actions on

Earth; I mean, how can you sort it all out the first time? So, just send me back and I will do it right. Eh? What's that? No? Outrageous! I'm no criminal!"

She moved closer to the radiant glow of soft, humming, swirling light. "What's that?" she said, vexed. "People like me create the path to everlasting torment with each thought and deed of our unrepentant heart? Well, I don't want to be with a vindictive God like Thee, after all; get me out of here, Thou can't talk to Margaret C. Carbuncle..."

The Tale Endeth

From where do fairy tales come?

Born, these tales, before or after the stories they fall from?

Well, reader, there is a fairy tale known to every child, which everyone seems to know, but no one seems to remember where it came from.

And it goes something like this:

Once upon a time there was this wicked old woman who hated everybody and everything in every way imaginable and even unimaginable, so naturally she became a principal of an elementary school; and she tortured the poor Teachers and secretaries and custodians and students and everyone else there in every devious way she could; but, in the end, she was defeated by the forces of Goodness and Justice, and the Teachers and students and everyone else there celebrated the wicked witch's grim death.

Schoolchildren especially love this story; and even some brave principals, with their nervous eyes on the door, will read "The Tale of the Wicked Principal" to classes.

There is a message at the end of this marvelous fairy tale, and it reads thusly: "Those who can, teach; those who cannot, become administrators."

PS And it's even worse if the Principal is a witch!

Fairy tales, they say, sometimes do come true.

—Finis—